Awkward Grace

By Jeff McCord

Twilight Times Books
Kingsport Tennessee

Awkward Grace

This is a work of fiction. All concepts, characters and events portrayed in this book are used fictitiously and any resemblance to real people or events is purely coincidental.

Copyright © 2008 by Jeff McCord.

All rights reserved. No part of this book may be reproduced, stored in a retrieval system or transmitted in any form by any means electronic, mechanical, photocopying, recording or otherwise, except brief extracts for the purpose of review, without the permission of the publisher and copyright owner.

Paladin Timeless Books
an imprint of
Twilight Times Books
P O Box 3340
Kingsport, TN 37664
www.twilighttimesbooks.com/

First edition, April 2008

Library of Congress Control Number: 2008009935

Cover art by Bryan Shackelford

Printed in the United States of America

For CeeGee

Acknowledgments

Without the help and guidance of Charles Gahari and his family, this novel would not have been possible. Thank you for making it better. And thank you for making me better.

CeeGee McCord and Grace McCord were the first to read this novel. My respect for these two women goes beyond my ability to describe. Thank you for your belief. It meant everything. Your corrections didn't hurt either.

In developing the characters for this novel, I borrowed liberally from the personality traits of Sam, Grace, and John McCord. There are none finer. Thank you for letting me try and paint a picture using your colors.

Any mistakes in history, culture, or nomenclature are completely my own. I had more than enough help to keep me from making them.

The Fifth Massacre

"Mevin, awake!" The hand was rough, uncharacteristically so. "Mevin, we must go. Wake your brother and Pierre. Then get dressed and wait." Mevin's father rushed from the room, leaving him dazed.

The late September rain banged down upon the metal roof, demanding to be let in. A constant vibration rattled through the small dwelling, creating a permanent intensity in Mevin's young heart. Nights brought no relief and sleep had to be snatched between the raindrops. The skies would not clear until April.

Mevin rose and crept to the two small figures piled within the same bed. His little brother Claude breathed lightly, but Pierre, the orphan, drew a deep desperate cadence. "Wake up, boys." Mevin's hand was gentle. "Wake up. We must go."

"What is it?" Pierre asked.

"I do not know. But I am afraid the Fifth Massacre has come."

༄༅

Mevin let his eyes open. The suddenness of a memory sometimes forced him to relinquish his hold on it. So he sat cross-legged on the wooden floor, his dark eyes floating across the four plank walls that housed him. Over the past six years, he'd take time like this occasionally, just to think and stare at the walls. But they held no answer, the walls that is. Mevin didn't blame them. It was unfair to ask a wall for answers. Handing out answers was not a wall's job. Still, he would come and think and stare, because just maybe one day an answer would appear. Maybe one day, like a painting or a window, an answer would hang upon on at least one of the bare walls. But in the meantime, he would think, and stare, and wait. In the September of the year 2000, that was how Mevin and his brother Claude lived their lives. Whether it be watching the walls or playing basketball on the dirt court down by the school building, everything was in the meantime. Their total existence was a wait. The West African nation of Burkina Faso provided them safe harbor, but no place to gain solid footing. And sooner or later, they would have to leave. To where was an answer that escaped both the walls' and the local officials' abilities to provide. But they'd have to go somewhere, because they couldn't live in a harbor, even a safe one, forever. So, sooner or later, they'd be traveling again. Maybe even back from where they had come.

Mevin blinked, and then closed his eyes again. It was hard to remember, really remember, the place from which he and Claude had come. But he felt the constant need to try. And when he tried, from somewhere amongst his father's stories, the cries at night from his brother's bed, and his own memory, Mevin was able to recall almost all of what had happened. He could not conjure the exact facts perhaps, but he'd come to believe that facts had more to do with specifics than with truth. Facts were the province of man. The truth lay in God's hands. And even though it seemed somehow apart from God, Mevin knew the truth.

ೞಛ

"Remy Gahutu! Remy Gahutu!" Pierre chanted the name as he rose from the bed and tried to pull on his pants.

"Remy Gahutu," Claude mumbled along with his friend, "Remy Gahutu."

"You boys hush and finish dressing. We must be ready when Father returns."

Mevin's father entered the room and pulled him aside. "Are the boys ready, Mevin?" He spoke Kirundi with a hushed and hurried tone. It was another oddity for Mevin's father, who insisted his sons speak the carefully metered French indicative of their schooling.

"Yes, Father we are ready. What is the matter?"

"The soldiers," the words coming so rapidly from Mevin's father sputtered and then stopped. Mevin stood within the charged silence waiting for them to continue. "Your mother. The soldiers have murdered your mother. They will be here. There is no time for tears. We must leave the hill at once."

Mevin's body shuddered. His stomach dropped and a dizziness gathered round him. He let go of an involuntary whimper, but, as his father instructed, he did not cry. The constancy of death dried his tears, and he drew courage from the steadfast sorrow upon which both he and his country were raised. But even in the midst of his bravery, Mevin's young heart knew it should not be that way. It was not the way courage was created. It was not the way God wanted it to be.

Soaking deep through their cotton clothes, the rain found the small party's skin immediately after they left their shelter. Mevin's father led, the two younger boys walked the middle, and Mevin took up the rear. They each carried a small pack stuffed with the barest provisions. Pierre did not want to leave, his voice rose in praise of Remy Gahutu, and he challenged Mevin's father to stay and fight like a man. Mevin's father shook the boy violently and commanded him to come along. Seeming more startled than afraid, Pierre obeyed. But now, Mevin worried that the boy would run into the brush in an attempt to hide and stay.

Mevin moved closer. "Pierre, you know we must leave. We have no weapons. We must go so that we may live."

"I do not wish to live. My mother is dead. My father is dead. I only wish to kill Tutsi. If I die, so be it."

The young boy's tone was old and defeated. There was no hope, no joy, no life. The voice of death took hold of his tongue. He spoke like a living fatality, as if the blood of Burundi had been drained directly from his own heart. Mevin thought the boy said something else, but the rain was too heavy to hear. He leaned closer to speak, but in an instant, his father was upon him.

"Hush, soldiers up ahead. Into the brush quickly. Quickly."

Mevin hustled the boys into the overgrowth and the three lay bellies down on the chocolate earth. Rain streamed off the hill and every once in a while the boys found it necessary to lift their bodies up in an effort to relieve the pools of water collecting at their sides. They lay for hours, and finally Mevin's heart slowed enough to consider his mother, let go of his courage, and weep. His sobs found a rhythm with the rain and for hours his sorrow sang out unknown to anyone, unheard by everyone.

When Mevin calmed down enough, he prayed. Jesus demanded no formality, so he made his plea in Kirundi. "God Almighty, Jesus Christ, Holy Spirit," his Anglican upbringing had taught him to address all three as one. "Please love Mother. Please wrap her in the peace of heaven. Help Claude and me make her proud. Help Father's heart to heal. Help us to escape. Save us from the soldiers."

Mevin's clothes stuck to his body like a soggy second skin. Mud caked his face, and the earth's odor forced his nostrils wide. As miserably uncomfortable as he was, fear and mourning still weakened his body. And reaching to find the hands of Claude and Pierre, he gave in to his fatigue and let his heavy eyes close.

ಬಂಡ

Memory faded into the present and again Mevin opened his eyes, stared at the walls and thought of his country. In Burkina Faso he had studied Burundi from afar, and he found it odd to be so academic about one's home. But he also found it somehow easier. To see Burundi as a place on the map, instead of a piece of his heart, muted his anguish. It did not give him peace really, only relief. But relief would do for now. For now, peace would have to wait. So sitting there, he thought of his country the way that his text books did.

The Central African nation of Burundi was a nation of hills. The people there called them hills, but impressed by their height, outsiders would likely call them mountains. Hill rolled upon hill, and narrow valleys filled with brush and overgrowth cut through the country-side like black snakes. Family-centered villages usually claimed a single hill as their own, and on that hill everyone knew one another. There was never a need for addresses or designations of kinship.

The people of Burundi were still primitive enough to honor family, to view it as a primal part of their lives. The Western text books that fed Mevin's studies seemed to find such a culture uncivilized. They labeled this strong affiliation to family as tribal, and there was more than a hint of disdain hidden within their dry academic language when describing it. But the more Mevin strayed from his text books and read works of fiction authored in those same Western countries, the more he found a longing from these civilized writers to restore that same sort of primacy of family to their own cultures. Their learning disparaged the notion of family while their literature constantly expressed the need for home and the yearning to belong there. To Mevin it was a strange paradox. Perhaps it was explainable in the difference between fact and truth, or even the temperaments of the academic and the heartfelt. Or maybe it was the gulf between relief and peace. He didn't know, and the walls held no answer. But the text books were certain. Such tribal tendencies led unerringly to horrific consequences. On this point, the facts were clear. And a point of proof was Remy Gahutu.

Depending on perspective, Remy Gahutu was either a freedom fighter or a murdering traitor. On any given subject, the world fostered many perspectives which in turn argued for the relativity of truth. But back in the fall of 1991, truth was not relative to Mevin. There was no argument as to the truth of Remy Gahutu. For Remy Gahutu was Hutu and so was Mevin.

Hutu was a description of background, but in order to relate it, Mevin thought ethnicity to be a better label. Mevin had read of the trouble in America over ethnicity, and though he did not know for sure, it also seemed that in the midst of the trouble there was hope. There seemed to be a truth in the fabric of that country which claimed that ethnicity was not the only way to judge a man. And so, there was the hope that one day the country would find this thread of truth. But there was no such claim in Burundi. At the time, a man's ethnicity was all that seemed to matter. For centuries, the Hutu had been persecuted by another ethnic group known as the Tutsi. It had always been bad, and there was almost no hope of it getting better. Four massacres had visited the Hutu at the hand of the Tutsi since the mid-1960s. The most tragic came in 1972, when a quarter of a million Hutu were murdered by their countrymen.

A quarter of a million, Mevin had a hard time comprehending such a number, and he supposed most other people did as well. Mevin's studies taught him that during that same time in 1972, the whole world watched the news coverage of a terrorist attack at the Munich Olympics. Around a dozen innocent people lost their lives in Munich. It was undeniably tragic, but Mevin wondered if any of those people watching their televisions in 1972 recalled a single word being said about the quarter of a million dead bodies lying about his country. He did not know for sure, and he did not like to dwell on such things.

He supposed that the people who decided what was tragic enough to show on the television had a hard job. They could not show everything. But while his classmates in Burkina Faso hungered for the television, Mevin had no taste for it.

During each of the massacres in Burundi, the Tutsi had controlled the military, so even though they were far fewer in number than the Hutu, they possessed the greater power to kill. So kill they did, and not without planning. First, they executed the Hutu army officers. Then they murdered high school students, businessmen, and people of means. Any Hutu with an education was a principal target. The only good educated Hutu was a dead educated Hutu.

Mevin knew that history was often at odds with first-hand accounts, most likely because those who wrote it were either trying to build reputations or bury skeletons. So it was not easy to gather an objective picture of what set off such a pattern of wickedness in Burundi, not for an historian and especially not for a person whose blood ran Hutu. But given enough distance and enough thought, a pretty good guess could be made.

There were basically two types of Tutsi—the Banyaruguru and the Hima. Their difference was well-known throughout all of Burundi. The Banyaruguru were the elite Tutsi, and they looked down upon the Hima. It was even said that a Banyaruguru Tutsi would rather marry a Hutu than a Hima Tutsi. There was constant struggle between these two groups. One kept trying to relegate the other to a lesser status and the other kept trying to shed the weight of its own inferiority. But the one thing the two groups did have in common was the fear that some morning the Hutu would wake up and, in the early light of day, realize that they could overwhelm their Tutsi masters, regardless of what type they were.

While there were not many who could claim to be an expert on the Burundian conflict, it did not take a professional historian to speculate that with a Hima Tutsi as president in 1972, it became in his best interest, and perhaps even made him feel less inferior, to rally both the Hima and Banyaruguru Tutsi behind a campaign of fear. It was a strategy that has made a habit of working in this world.

Mostly, the Hutu fell beneath the Tutsi machete without resistance, but in later years, Remy Gahutu and his men struck back at the Tutsi army. Killing government soldiers and raiding Tutsi villages, Gahutu's actions claimed a boldness not typical of Hutu. Anxiety swelled among both the Hima and the Banyaruguru. And in 1991, after three decades and four massacres, the Tutsi once again rallied behind fear.

Mevin's father stayed through it all. Educated in Belgium and an adviser in the agricultural ministry, his risks in staying were higher than most. But when friends fled to Rwanda, he stayed. When the murders reached the next hill over, he stayed. Even when moderate Tutsi colleagues secretly pleaded with him to go, he stayed. "This is our home," he told Mevin. "One does not abandon his home. Without home, there is no life." But that night, they were indeed abandoning their home. Into the dark and the rain, they had fled, away from home, away from life.

Mevin convinced his eyes to close again.

※※

The soldiers searched through the night. Their orders were to dispose of specific targets and the consequence of failure was always uncertain. Finding the woman was lucky and quick. But, they could not find the man or the children. Word of their arrival must have spread quickly, and it angered them to the point of rage. Finally, near dawn they knocked upon the door of a small house on the edge of the hill. When a man answered the door, they shot him in the head. Entering the home, they dragged two frightened children from their beds and hacked them with machetes until the bloody chunks of their little bodies were indistinguishable from the cakes of mud around them. The soldiers returned to the dead man and hacked him up as well. After casually discussing rape, they determined the night's work had rendered them too exhausted. So they left the woman in the house alone. The soldiers had already killed their one woman. They needn't expend the energy to kill another. And because of her fortune, they told the woman that she was lucky.

A wail of desperate hysteria leapt from the lucky woman, cut through the rain, and fell upon the ears of Mevin's father who had been hiding within sight of the massacre. The woman would go mad. This was a certainty. Mevin's father had seen it many times before. Resisting the urge to turn away, he watched until exhausted by her tears, the lucky woman lay motionless on the muddy ground. And later, when he would recount the event to Mevin, he would hesitate and say, "I feel I need to protect you from the truth. But I feel stronger that if one is protected from the truth, he is defenseless against lies."

ಬಂಡ

The rain continued its jealous rhythm, and no ray of sunshine broke across the hill. But darkness ebbed and morning, though sodden and meek, rose through the sky.

"Mevin. Wake the boys and gather your packs."

Mevin's father leaned in close to him. Grief filled his steady brown eyes, their usual clarity blurred by a film of anguish. Once seemingly too strong to shed tears, now Mevin was uncertain whether they would ever be dry.

"The soldiers?" Mevin asked.

"The soldiers are gone. They are no longer looking for us."

"Can we return home?"

"No. Home is no longer Burundi. Evil has stolen her. We must go. At least for a while, we must go and wait for Burundi to return."

"Go where, father?"

"To Rwanda."

The Call

There was a place where the rugged beauty of the land soaked through the souls of those who walked upon it. There was a place where cautious introductions gave way to an unfaltering depth of caring. There was a place where handshakes were firm, smiles were honest, and a friend meant your very life. It was a place of hills and valleys. And it was a place that understood life like the land was made of both. People from outside the place called it clannish and even backward. They did not understand it, though they were certain they did. But their perceptions failed to change the nature of the place. Its truth had always weathered perception.

Ben Bellamy knew this place, not in his mind or even in his heart, but deep down beyond the location where words gather and emotions are born. Ben knew this place in his soul. And to him, the best part about this place was that it was real. It was a real live place. The place was called East Tennessee, and he had never lived in another place. He didn't see a reason to. This was the place, and though it was September of the year 2000, it might as well had been forever.

"Dad! Dad! Telephone… Dad!"

"Down here, Puckett."

At the sound of Ben's voice, the little boy took off like a shot. Clunking down the porch steps in his blue canvas cowboy boots, he skidded momentarily across the gravel driveway before finding his balance. "Dad?"

"Down here, buddy. I'm down here."

Ben watched Puckett scan the fence row for the shape of his body. He lay next to a wild blackberry bush tangled in a swarm of barbed-wire and eventually Puckett's eyes lit upon his calamity. The little boy hurried down to help.

"What happened, Dad?"

"Oh nothing. I was just running a little wire and got tangled up. This stuff comes off the roll ready to bite you."

"You're bleeding."

"Oh it's nothing. I'll be all right in a minute. Why don't you hand me those fencing pliers lying on the post up there. I can't hardly get up to reach them."

Puckett stretched his three foot frame mightily, but just couldn't get a grasp.

"Try shaking the post buddy," Ben suggested.

With a thin-armed shove, the boy rocked the post just slightly. But it was enough. The fencing pliers teetered on the rounded edge and then fell. Bouncing off the fence's top strand, the metal tool accelerated downward and struck Ben heavily above the right eyebrow. Ben felt the beginnings of a good-sized egg pushing down toward his eyelid and he knew from a wealth of experience the spot would soon be turning an ugly yellowish purple.

"I'm sorry, Dad."

"Oh it's not your fault, buddy," Ben said smiling through the soft throbbing over his eye. "I shouldn't have been looking up at the post like that. It's nothing anyway. I'll be all right in a minute. Here we go. That's it." He cut the wire away from his tattered, blood soaked jeans only to reveal that his ankles were shredded and his left knee sported a three inch gash. "Free," he said as he stood. "Good as new."

Puckett eyed him honestly, "I don't think so Dad. You look like you've been in a fight."

"That's what we'll tell your mama—a terrible fight with a wild pig."

"She won't believe you, Dad."

"Hey, when did you start with all this Dad business? What happened to Daddy?"

"I'm getting big, Dad."

"I know you are. Who is on the phone?"

"I don't know. They didn't say."

"Well, let's go see if they've given up on us yet." Ben removed his leather glove, reached down to take his son's hand and the two walked back to the small planked house without much hurry.

Benjamin Alvin Bellamy was born a mixed blessing. A tall, sturdily built man; he combined an enormously high tolerance for pain with an uncanny aptitude for injury. It had always been that way. Growing up Ben was never awkward or clumsy, far from it. He thought of himself as always being at least functionally athletic. But there was something about the way he walked through the world. It was as if pain liked to take a shot at him just because he was so hard to hurt. Ben's neighbor, Joe Shelton, told him that mixed blessings made for enlightening Greek tragedies and good country music songs, but that it was an awful tough way to make a harmony in real life. Ben shrugged it all off. It was what it was. And in the end, when it was all added up, it was pretty darn good. Still, as he walked along with Puckett's hand in his, he was glad mixed blessings weren't hereditary.

ঞ৩

The phone line in the kitchen was dead, no big surprise. It had taken a good ten minutes to cut loose from the wire.

"Didn't say who it was huh?"

"No sir, just that he needed to speak to you right now."

"Right now?"

"Yes sir, right now."

"That's kindly rude don't you think?"

"Yes sir, I think."

The phone rang, startling them both. "Well, maybe he's back."

"Maybe."

"Hello."

"Ben Bellamy?"

"Yes, this is Ben Bellamy."

The voice was smooth, not sweet smooth, salesman smooth. There was also an amused quality about it, not joyful amused, condescending amused. Ben recognized it right off.

"Let me suggest something to you, son. Don't let a child answer the telephone. I called earlier and was waiting for thirty minutes after that child of yours answered the phone."

"Who is this?" Ben said smiling down at Puckett.

"This is Pastor Lumpkin."

"Well hello, Pastor. It wasn't Puckett's fault. It was mine. I got myself mixed up with some barbed wire, and…"

"Spare the rod and spoil the child. That's all I have to say on the matter. Spare the rod and spoil the child." The pastor released a soft chuckle.

"Why are you calling?"

Eloise Bellamy entered the kitchen with the first-aid kit as Ben felt a flash of frustration rise through his countenance. It took a lot to raise Ben's ire, something even pushy telemarketers almost never did. Eloise gave him a quick peck on the cheek and then, while he talked, examined his wounded face.

"I need you to do something for me, Ben."

"What would that be, Pastor Lumpkin?"

At the name, Eloise gave Ben a quizzical look and began cleaning the abrasion which sat atop the purple mountain now closing his right eye. At her touch, Ben's whole body softened, and his voice gathered its naturally kind tone.

"I need outreach at First Communion. We are called to be fishers of men, and I need someone with a boat. Do you get my meaning, Ben?"

"All I've got is that ten-foot john boat out back," Ben's grin broke broadly toward his wife and son. "But you know I'd be happy to let you borrow it any time."

"I'm not talking about a boat, son. I'm talking in a parable, like Jesus. I guess I'll have to explain it, like you were my disciple."

"Oh no. That's okay, Pastor. I think I get your meaning. The church needs someone to do some outreach work."

"No. No. I need someone to head an outreach committee. And you're the one who is going do it."

Ben gave a long pause and looked at Eloise. His wife was beautiful. He worried because she stayed so thin, but that did nothing to mute his attraction for her. Her long red hair and green eyes made him sigh. She'd grown up in First Communion, and he ought not turn from an opportunity to serve the church.

"I'll tell you what, Pastor. Let me talk to Eloise, and I'll call you back in the morning."

"Don't let me down, son."

"Yes sir. Goodbye now." Ben cradled the phone softly.

"You know, you really need to go see a doctor about this. I'm serious this time." Eloise lifted Ben's leg, forcing him to sit down on the pine bench next to the breakfast table. Rubbing-alcohol in hand, she began cleaning the cuts around his ankles. "What did the pastor have to say?"

Letting the doctor comment pass, Ben attended to the question instead. "Oh, he wants me to head up some kind of outreach committee over at the church."

"Are you going to do it?"

Ben let this question lay as he surveyed his kitchen. It was his Grandmother Catherine's kitchen, actually. She'd left the house and farm to him; there were no other family, so he got it all. The room was polished pine, with a full grain and an occasional knot. Catherine had been raised in Valdosta, Georgia, and she'd loved the pines. Her one complaint about East Tennessee had been that there were too many hardwoods.

"I wonder why Granny Catherine never went back to Valdosta."

"I don't know, Sweetheart." Eloise finished what she could and said, "You're gonna have to take off these boots and then your pants. You might as well toss those jeans out. They're in ribbons." Turning to Puckett she said, "You go on and get a bath, baby. Soon as you get out, we'll have our supper."

"Yes ma'am. Can I take my army men?"

"Yes you can. But get them out of the tub when you're done. I just hate it when I sit down on one of those things."

"I will," Puckett promised and then clunked off to wage a clean war.

"I guess I'm going to do it." Ben stripped down to his boxers.

"I thought you might."

"Lumpkin won't be one bit of help."

"Shush now, Ben. It's not like you to bad-talk anybody. And besides, you're speaking of the Pastor."

"I know Eloise, but the man can't even throw a baseball. Have you ever seen him? He doesn't even know that he's doing it wrong or has no shame one. The man throws like a girl."

"I'm glad Granny Catherine's not around to hear you talk like that."

"Well, I guess you're right. It'd be better to say that he throws like most girls."

"I'm not sure why that matters anyway."

"I'm not sure either."

Ben removed his shirt without prompting, allowing Eloise to examine his back for wounds. "You look all right back here, nothing but that old scar," she said, referring to a relic from the only real fight Ben had ever had. "I'm done with you. Go jump in the tub with Puckett before he runs all the hot water out."

"Can I take my army men?"

"Go on," she said shooing him with a smile. "I've got supper to fix."

Catherine Bellamy had built the two-bedroom farmhouse in Mount Carmel, Tennessee with her husband, Earl. The two met at a Christian missionary convention in Atlanta. Neither one had ever been out of the country. Neither were even officially missionaries, but they felt oddly called to attend the convention. One accidental meeting later, and they both knew why. That was the story anyway.

Catherine had a big family, so the wedding was in Valdosta. But Earl's work and a forty-acre piece of land were back in Mount Carmel. So they'd come home, and tragedy soon joined them. Their first daughter died of meningitis at four years old. Their second daughter died at seventeen giving birth to Ben. It was too much for Earl. Grief took him later that same year. And though she must have yearned for it, Catherine didn't die. It seemed she just decided not to. Ben's biological father was thirty-two and already married with three children when he'd convinced Ben's sixteen-year-old mother that he loved her. He moved his wife and family to Knoxville at the first hint of her pregnancy. Ben had nobody else worth mentioning. For the boy to have a chance at life, Catherine couldn't die. That seemed to be enough to make her live, at least for a while. And while she lived, it was with a vigor. More than Ben was blessed by her existence, and more than Ben missed her badly when she decided that it was finally okay to pass on.

Supper was eaten at a leisurely pace. There was a lot of food, but Eloise's boys cleaned their plates. After the dishes were washed and put away, Puckett fed the dogs while Ben went to lock down the barn. The two met back up by the creek where Puckett liked to listen to the bullfrogs.

"They sound a little sore throated this evening."

"Yes sir, they do. Hey Dad, I've been thinking."

"Thinking is a good thing."

"Well, I've been thinking. And I think I'm about ready for a little brother."

"Is that right?" Ben didn't try to conceal his grin.

"I'm serious, Dad. Don't you think it's about the right time?"

"Well Puckett, I'm still practicing being a dad on you. I never had one of my own so I don't quite know how to go about it."

"Ahhh, you're doing just fine, Dad."

"Well all the same, I'd like a little more practice before I go on and get ahead of myself."

"Well, think about it."

"I'll do that."

Ben had thought about it. And though he fretted over his own aptitude as a father, it wasn't the only reason for his reluctance. Puckett's birth had been rough on Eloise, and Ben couldn't bear the thought of his own mother's story coming full circle while trying to have a second child. One child with two parents was fine for now. Maybe later, God willing, things might even up.

Even on a good evening, bullfrogs could only hold an audience for so long. Ben and Puckett meandered back to the house, stopping here and there to wrestle a little. Along the way, an errant tree stump made acquaintance with Ben's right shin. He toppled heavily into a black walnut tree, jamming his shoulder before sliding down its trunk. Gathering himself, he jumped up quickly.

"You okay, Dad?"

"I'll be all right in a minute. No problem at all."

Ben brushed himself off and then squatted to eye-level with Puckett. "Do me a favor, buddy. Don't tell your mama."

They found Eloise rocking on the front porch swing. Ben eased down beside her, finding the swing's cadence without breaking the silence. "We are so blessed," Eloise whispered over the soft creak of their motion.

The September sun sank behind the hills and color burned in muted tones across the East Tennessee sky. Eloise spread a cotton blanket over her legs and laid her head upon Ben's shoulder. He smelled her hair and felt the peace of a good marriage. They watched their son running with the two chocolate lab mixes that were more trouble than they were good. The bath with the army men was long past being useful, and little boy laughter bounced off the outbuildings, on toward the hills, and up, up, to heaven.

"Yes we are," Ben said softly. "We are truly blessed."

False Liberty

A creak came from one of the floor boards just outside the room, causing Mevin to look away from the walls and toward the door. From his seated position he listened, his entire being focused on hearing even the slightest movement. Claude was not due back for over an hour, but Mevin was cautious. He did not want his younger brother to find him sitting and staring at the walls. Claude would not understand. It would upset him. So, Mevin listened until he was sure that the sound had been born of its own accord. Then he let his eyes drift from the door and back to the walls. And upon them, he saw a camp in Rwanda.

In 1991, a Rwandan refugee camp was a place where parents buried their children one-by-one until they were all gone, a place where children lost their parents to become slaves to others, a place where, for most people, the only solace was the knowledge that life ended. There was no clothing, no education, no hope. Digging graves was the only honest work available. A Rwandan refugee camp was where the dead pretended to live.

Camps were typically huge plots of land without fences and set up far away from population centers. Usually, they were close to some kind of road and near a river. There were no houses in the camps, only Red Cross or UNHCR (United Nations High Commissioner for Refugees) trailers. Most people slept in small white tents scattered upon the bare grassless ground. Not everybody had a tent. There were never enough, and the UNHCR gave priority to families with two or more children. For those left without, plastic sheeting was used as make-shift shelters to keep the rainy seasons at bay. When the rains came hard, the inhabitants of tents and plastic sheeting held their belongings up off the ground to protect them from the muck that oozed under their dwellings.

Living conditions bred disease. And when the UNCHR trucks arrived to deliver clean drinking water, the feeble were often unable to push their way through the thirsty lines. Many died of dehydration. Hunger was constant and yellow corn powder, like the kind used to feed cattle, was often the only source of food. Medicine was rarely available. Fevers raged and babies died. Mevin's family set out in search of such a camp. And on a rainy day they found one.

Even from afar, the camp looked like a muddy clump of despair. Figures moved about the tents with slumped shoulders. Large groups of men gathered in silence for no apparent reason. The wail of sick children filled the air with a musical intensity, and the smell of sweat and urine lifted upon the wind as a warning to passersby.

This was Mevin's escape, his salvation. He, along with Claude, Pierre and his father had managed to avoid various groups of soldiers on their cross-country trek in a quest for life. But they had found no life, only death's holding pen.

"I'd rather be dead," Pierre hissed. "This is a coward's place. We will die in this place like sheep. It is better to die in Burundi than live like this." Pierre was careful to keep his comments out of earshot of Mevin's father who was busy negotiating for a tent.

Mevin turned on the younger boy but found himself unable to speak. Pierre seemed much older, and Mevin could not muster the intensity to scold him.

"You mustn't speak those words," a dark, round woman said, wandering into their conversation from out of the desolate crowd.

"They are words of truth," Pierre protested.

"No. They are words of bitterness," the woman corrected softly. "They are the words of the Israelites."

"Do not speak some Bible story to me. Look at this place. God does not live here," Pierre spat back.

"God does not live here," Claude said, mumbling his allegiance.

"Hush." Mevin scolded his brother, and then gaining momentum, "Both of you. Hush that talk. It is bad talk." Turning to the woman, he continued, "I am sorry. We are very hungry and very tired. Of course, we know that God is everywhere. Even here."

The dark, round woman observed the boys through the deep creases of her face. "He is here. He is not easy to find, but He is here. You must look especially hard when evil is about. But do not stop looking. Here, to look is to live.

"My name is Anna. We have no preacher here, but I am the Bible teacher. We will have prayer tonight and every night. Tell your father to come and see."

Anna wandered back into the crowd just as Mevin's father returned. "We have a tent," he said with relief. "It is not big, but it is a tent. Come and see."

They survived, and they waited. For weeks, then months, that was all they did. Mevin grew desperate for school. He fretted over falling behind. He felt ignorance seeping through his pores like a sickness. He worried that his chance for knowledge had passed, and he feared the loss of his craving for it.

Mevin's father would not let the boys pout. "The difference," he told Mevin, "between routine and drudgery is belief. We must believe that this will end. We must believe that this is only a part of our purpose. We must know that we are Joseph. Today, we are powerless to stand against the betrayal of our brothers. Tomorrow, we are strong enough to save their lives. Believe, Mevin. And help Claude and Pierre to believe as well."

They ate better than most. Mevin's father had cousins in Burkina Faso. During the periods of calm in Burundi, Mevin's father had earned a good living. He'd helped his relatives, and in their country's peace, they found success. Now they sent money. By instruction, it was never very much. Thieves were thick, and Mevin also had the feeling that his father did not want to ask for too much, at least not now. In addition to corn powder, they exchanged cash for beans and cassava. And sometimes, they were even able to buy fish. Mevin lived his days standing in line for drinking water and re-reading his Bible, the single book he had taken from the hill.

Most evenings found the group gathered around Anna's tent for Bible class. But on Tuesdays, Mevin's father took leave and assembled with other men to speak of Hutu and Tutsi. The majority of men spoke in fanciful scenarios of death and destruction to the whole of Tutsi kind. No amount of carnage seemed unwarranted. Pierre never attended Bible study on Tuesdays, but Mevin and Claude could often hear the men arguing on the way back from Anna's tent.

"How can you say that?" came a stranger's raspy demand. "What of your wife and your home? What of your neighbors?"

Then the soft, metered, voice of Mevin's father countered, "The killing will not stop until we choose a different way. Fear and evil have run us from our homes, not the Tutsi. We must not add sticks to a fire of fear and evil."

"You are crazy," raucous laughter drowned out the soft voice. "The Tutsi will not allow peace. They must die."

Each night before bed, Mevin led a prayer for health. "Father, watch over us. Make us well and clean. Keep us from sickness. Do not let a fever come upon us. Make our water pure and our bodies sound, in the name of the Father, Son, and Holy Spirit. Amen."

"Also make us strong," Pierre would inevitably add when he showed enough interest.

Mevin abandoned the stern look he'd once used to admonish the boy. He did not want to engage in some sort of staring contest; a test of wills he knew Pierre would win. As weeks passed, he found it increasingly difficult to hold Pierre's gaze at all. Mevin felt his brother's friend slipping farther away. To where, he did not know.

⊱⊰

Mevin's eyes had been closed. He did not remember willing them to do so. He thought perhaps he had fallen asleep. But his thoughts had been too clear to call them a dream. So he sighed and for a moment thought about Rwanda with open eyes.

For two years, the group waited, listened, and tried to believe. Mevin and the other boys grew, but not as boys should. Their souls were bathed in death and they became accustomed to it. Everyday abominations made the notion of atrocity seem almost casual. But now Mevin knew that there was no such thing as a casual atrocity. Babies that vomit themselves to death demanded a relentless outrage. But after witnessing atrocity after atrocity, it wore a callus on their souls. It was not the atrocity that lessened, only the feel of it. A calloused soul was no soul at all. A boy's soul ought to be a gift freely given, not something to be protected like an injured bird. But circumstance gave what ought to be a very hard time. And so given the circumstance, with the help of Anna, Mevin's father tried hard to protect them. But as Mevin let his eyes close again, he was overcome by the thought that even as she sings her morning song, a mother bird knows that not all her chicks will survive. And Mevin's father must have known that as well.

Early on a dry-season day, the camp awoke with a buzz. The news of the election spread smiles across ravaged faces. Hope drifted from tent to plastic sheeting and back to tent again. Incredible as it seemed, a Hutu had been elected president of Burundi. Home seemed less distant. Belief swelled.

"See, I told you to believe," Mevin chastised Claude and Pierre. "Now we have a Hutu president. All will be okay."

In June 1993, the Burundian government bowed to international pressure, especially strong from the United States, and held its first free elections. Melchior Ndadaye won the election with sixty-five percent of the vote. Melchior Ndadaye was a Hutu. He became the first ruler from the country's ethnic majority in its history.

Mevin burst through the opening of the tent and found his father seated. "We can return home, Father. The Tutsi are no longer our masters. We have won! We have won! When will we return home?"

Mevin's father smiled slightly. "It is a great victory. It is good to be alive in times of great victory. But we will wait a while before returning home. Sometimes, victory must happen more than once before it is final."

Mevin frowned. He found his father's calm unimaginable. Joy rang through his own heart. Home tasted fresh. Life felt tangible. It was time to go home and to live. He could not comprehend his father's composure.

"Don't let me ruin the day for you, Son. It is a great victory and deserves to be celebrated. But for now, we will wait. We will wait and see if our home has truly returned to us."

The dry season waned, and the rains fell. Hope stirred, and families began leaving the camp with the dream of reclaiming their homes. But hope had a fragile root, and in October of 1993, it was pulled from the Hutu again. On October 21, Melchior Ndadaye was tortured to death by Tutsi officers of the

Burundian military. Ndadaye heard rumors of an assassination plot but didn't believe them. His faith was in democracy and the fidelity of his countrymen. His last words were said to be, "Think of the people, your families. Do not spill the blood." But his plea went unheeded, and the blood spilled.

On October 22, wholesale killing of Hutu erupted in rural areas. And in the capital city, targeted murders, mostly in the neighborhoods that had voted in large numbers for Ndadaye, fell upon the populace. The Hutu fought back and in the end, over 150,000 bodies lay about the small country in mockery of faith and fidelity.

The news of Ndadaye's death hit the camp like a bomb. Mournful wails echoed hope's escape. The whole camp became listless. Men and women lay about the tents, stunned. Children's cries went unanswered. Even hunger subsided in deference to despair.

Mevin found his father sitting in the tent. "Father, what shall we do?"

"I have no answer for you. Only that first we must mourn and then we must believe. Do you understand?"

"Yes father," Mevin said, though not understanding at all.

His father opened his arms and Mevin went to him. He cried and his father let him. When the tears subsided, his father said, "Go find Claude and Pierre. We will stay close to our tent today."

Mevin searched the camp thoroughly, even going to the sections forbidden by his father. On the road and by the river, he willed his eyes to see two small figures. But by nightfall, he knew. He could not force himself to return to his father's tent with the news. So Mevin looked on through the gathering darkness until his father found him.

"Mevin?"

"They are gone, Father. Claude and Pierre are gone."

The Gate

Joe Shelton limped in the mornings. He wasn't a limper later in the day, but in the mornings he had a tendency to drag his hip a little, or maybe it was his knee. He wasn't quite sure. He just knew that the pain caused him to ease his stride and move a little slower when the sun was still young. If he'd wanted he could have slept later, or at least stayed within the warmth of the house until the stiffness in his leg subsided. Joe had no place to go, really. Over his long life, he'd already gone everywhere he needed to go, both in his travels and in his craft. So, there was no practical reason to get up early and even less of one to go outside. But nobody had ever called Joe a practical man.

Of course Joe knew why he got up early. And if not exactly practical, it was sensible; at least it was to Joe. Every person he had ever come to know spent at least a piece of their life's time looking for some sort of passageway. In some cases, it was spiritual in nature, and in others, it was no more than a means to try and touch a time gone by. But be it prayer or plastic surgery, everybody seemed to be looking for a way to get through the fences that surrounded them. Joe was no different, and he didn't pretend to be. But Joe was lucky, or better said, he was blessed. And after decades of listening for the words that would make a song worth writing, he was good at knowing the places where a good word was likely to show up. Words had always been Joe's passageway, and the best kind he had ever found lay just over the hill. Tolerating an early morning limp seemed a small price to pay.

"You sold any cows yet, boy?"

"Not lately. You written any songs, Old Man?"

"Not lately."

Come rain or shine, every morning Joe met Ben at the gate between their farms. Their barns sat within a stone's throw of each other, and on a farm, visits to the barn were as regular as a heartbeat. But if Joe was being honest, which he had a hard time not being, he'd have to say that their meetings had less to do with the barns and more to do with the heart.

Ben hadn't sold a cow since Catherine Bellamy had died. He never told Joe the exact reason. But after a loss, Joe supposed a person tried to hold onto what was left—at least the kind-hearted ones did. Ben ordered bull sperm from the Co-op and used some turkey-baster looking contraption to bring the calves along. He kept them all. He made the bull calves into steers to keep the herd honest, but he wouldn't let a single one go. It made for a fine looking group of Herefords, none of which were for sale.

"Your cows are getting some age on them. What are you going to do when they start dying off? Don't want to spend all your time digging cow holes."

"I'll just cross that bridge when I come to it. But how about you? Your songs are getting some age on them. What are you going to do when the royalties peter out? Can't spend all your time just figuring on the next good song."

Joe Shelton was not a household name, never had been. Even in their primes, most songwriters never laid claim to household names. But there was a time in Nashville, Austin, and even Los Angeles when a Joe Shelton crafted song meant gold to an entertainer. That time had passed, but the folks who knew said it was only because Joe let it.

"I guess I'll cross that bridge when I come to it, too."

Every morning they started their talks the same way. Sometimes it would be about all they'd say. But most times, they'd say more. Women, not men, were known for talking. A man wasn't as likely to commune in that way. Joe figured it was because a man and a woman were different, mostly due to the fact that a man wasn't as smart. Like a woman, a man needed to talk, to hear words and to say words, but a man just wasn't smart enough to know how to get started. So, Joe and Ben relied on cows and songs to get them started. The more Joe considered it, the more he thought the whole sentiment to be a solid idea for a song in its own right.

"The preacher called yesterday."

They'd waited a minute or two in silence to see if a talk would take. Joe was glad it did. "What did old Pastor Lumpkin have to say?"

"He said he needed me to start an outreach program for him."

"For him?"

"Yes sir. He's a piece of work, isn't he?"

"Don't let a pastor get in the way of doing the Lord's work."

"Oh, I'll probably do it. But that fella, I don't know, Joe. I just need to shut up about it. But have you ever seen him throw a baseball?"

"Yes I have. He throws like a girl doesn't he? Doesn't even seem to bother him, either."

"I know. It just flies all over me. And I don't even know why. I don't know why it should even matter. It's dumb for it to matter. Don't you think?"

"Maybe, maybe not. It speaks to his upbringing. When he was a boy, nobody must have taken the initiative to show him how to throw a ball proper. His father was a preacher, too, wasn't he?"

"I believe so."

"So maybe his father was too busy saving souls to teach the boy to reach back and follow through. Maybe his father didn't even know how to throw. Maybe he told the boy that knowing how to throw wasn't important. Folks like to think what they know how to do is important. They tend to look down upon the things that they're no good at. The fact that nobody taught him to throw a baseball as a boy may say a lot about the man he grew up to be, or it may say nothing at all."

"I suspect it says a lot."

"I suspect you're right."

The silence came back upon them as they retreated into their own thoughts. "Hey, Joe," Ben said suddenly, "Granny Catherine taught me to throw, but how did she learn?"

The memory made Joe laugh, and Ben smiled at him while he reigned in his chuckle. "I taught her," Joe managed to say. "And that woman could really bring it."

"You taught her?"

"Yep. I taught her so she could teach you."

"Why didn't you just teach me?"

"Your grandmother was an amazing woman, Ben. And you are fortunate to have her blood. Even though she'd never been taught herself, she was wise enough to consider that a boy needed to know. She figured that I could show you, but that wasn't going to cut it. Her reason for living was to raise you. I suspect she thought that if she gave away any of that responsibility, it may chip away at the reason. So I taught her to teach you. And, Lord knows, we had fun. She'd rear back in that long skirt of hers and fireball it faster than any man I ever knew. I'd rub my hand and she'd laugh and laugh. I loved to hear your grandmother laugh. She was a good one. And she was the right one to teach you. She was a lot better than I ever thought of being."

Ben listened kindly. Joe had always admired the way Ben listened. His way was to make a person feel good about what they were saying, let them talk and enjoy the sound of their own voice. Folks liked the sound of their own voice, and Ben always gave a person the feeling that he liked it, too. After Joe finished his talking, another question rose in Ben's eyes, and it just about made it to his mouth when he slipped off the post he'd propped himself against. Head-first, he fell right into six strands of rusty wire. It cut his forehead wide open.

"Dang, boy, are you all right? That's got to hurt."

"Oh I'll be all right in a minute," Ben said pushing himself off the ground and to his knees. "That wire is bad to bite you."

Joe stepped through the fence and trotted to Ben's barn. Eloise kept a large first-aid kit mounted inside the second stall. It was well supplied, and Joe quickly found what he needed. He doctored him up good. He had plenty of practice. It wasn't the first time.

"You're looking good, boy."

"Thanks, Old Man."

They stood in silence for a while. "Well, I better get rolling. Lou likes to get started on time." Ben gave in to a small smile.

"Yeah. I bet that's true. Off with you, then. Have a good day." Joe had a strong notion to give Ben a hug. It snuck up on him like that from time to time. But Joe had never been much of a hugger. He didn't have anything against it. He just didn't know how exactly to go about it. They shook hands, and Joe watched Ben walk into his barn. Not once did Ben tend to his forehead. Joe could almost hear pain curse its failure, and for a moment he wondered if he could find a decent rhyme for "failure". And then just as quickly, his thoughts turned to Lou.

Lou was short for Louise. Louise was Ben's sister-in-law which meant she was Eloise's sister. "Louise" and "Eloise", it was their father's doing. Joe saw that as proof that a man shouldn't be allowed to name his daughters. But still, names had a way of working themselves out. The name "Lou" matched Miss Louise better than her father could have imagined.

༄༅

Ben pulled his aging Ford F150 next to the battered Silverado, took a long pull on his coffee, and rolled down his window. Merle Haggard's voice faded from the Chevy beside him and a pony-tailed redhead leaned out. "What'd you do to your forehead, honey?"

"Oh nothing really. Me and the fence just got acquainted this morning."

"If you get any more acquainted with that fence, you'll have to propose."

Ben gave her a wry smile. "I do think your sister is getting a little worried about the relationship."

Lou rumbled from the truck and propped herself against Ben's Ford. She was built like an oak, tall and solid. Although wide at the shoulders like a man, it was still more than obvious that she was a woman. Even through a flannel shirt and baggy dungarees, the long curves of her body gave its gender away. There was a time when folks would've called her a good birthing woman, but never to her face.

"Well, don't just sit there smiling like a fool. We've got a job site to look over before the crew decides to show up."

"Yes, ma'am. I'm coming right now." Ben smiled again. He couldn't help himself. Everything Lou said tickled him. He loved his wife's older sister. It was an honest love, a humorous love. Lou was family, and when afforded the opportunity, Ben took strongly to family.

They were roofers—Ben and Lou that is. The two became partners shortly after Ben and Eloise married. Both learned under Lou's father, but Lou mastered the craft better than Ben. Ben was better skilled than most, but Lou was better skilled than everyone. Ben fared better with the customers. No matter how good she could lay a shingle, a short-tempered, red-headed, female roofer was a good reason for most folks to look for another roofer. The truth was that they probably would have starved without each other. Together, they were known for being the best roofers in the region. Word-of-mouth traveled all the way to Bristol and on to Johnson City, but most of their jobs were in Kingsport. A nice living was a blessing, and Ben knew that he and Lou were doubly blessed.

The two were laying metal shingles with their crew on a big house in the Fair Acres neighborhood. It paid well but took the skill of a craftsman. So on that day, Ben and Lou did most of the work along with one of the more experienced crew members, while the others fed them materials, watched, and learned. Lou's flannel shirt and dungarees were her uniform. Even when the heat rose, she stayed true to it. Red-headed and fair skinned, it was easy to suppose she covered so as not to burn. But there was probably more to it than that. It was easy to see that Lou's femininity was not a comfort to her. Being noticed for it made her squirm. She outworked any man on any day, but when the sun lay down she was a big, tall, beautiful woman. It seemed a tough truth for her to reconcile. Ben required the crew to also wear shirts and long pants. It was one of those little things that made the customers happy. And it also left Lou with nothing to explain.

The day stayed cool and the cloud cover muted the view of Bays Mountain. The crew worked steadily with the rhythmic progress of a job well-done.

"Hey Lou," Ben said breaking the cadence.

"Hey what?"

"Do you know how to throw a baseball?"

"Do I know how to do what?"

"Throw a baseball."

"Honey, I can throw a baseball farther than any man on this roof."

Three local boys worked beside them. All but one had been with the crew for over a year, and the bowed heads of his buddies told the new man to keep quiet in the face of a physical challenge from Lou. But Ben wasn't having it. He raised up to defy his sister-in-law.

"I can throw a baseball…" That was all he got out before his feet abandoned him. Taking one big bounce on his backside, Ben popped off the metal roof like a champagne cork and into the waiting arms of a blue princess holly bush. Even the new boy had seen him go many times before. All hands scurried down the ladder after him.

Lou stopped by the F150 to grab the first-aid kit Eloise kept mounted near the passenger-side door. But by the time she joined the others, the boys were laughing and headed back toward the ladder.

"Jimney Christmas, Ben, you've got to stop doing that. One of these days it's going to be more than a couple of scratches. One of these days you're going to get yourself hurt. Are you sure you don't need to go see a doctor, honey?"

"Oh it's nothing. I'll be all right in a minute. But one of these days we're going to find ourselves a baseball and test out that redheaded pride of yours."

"Ben honey, what is it with you and the baseball. You nearly killed yourself, and you still come up talking about throwing a baseball. I think you have an inner-ear problem. You really need to go see a doctor."

They climbed the ladder in silence and started back to work. Ben usually had only one brush with death each day, so now that it was over the crew's nerves seemed to settle quickly.

"I'm glad we got that out the way early," Lou whispered.

"What's that?" Ben asked.
"Nothing, honey. Nothing at all."
"Who taught you to throw?"
"What?"
"Who taught you to throw a baseball?"
"Come off the baseball stuff, we have shingles to lay."
"No, really."
Lou paused and looked over the crew's progress. "No one."
"What?"
"No one taught me to throw a baseball. I've just always known. Ever since I can remember, I could chuck it a mile. In first grade, they used to call me Ellie May."
"But somebody must have showed you. Your dad maybe?"
"Nope. I've just always known how. It's always been a part of me, sort of like my uncanny ability to scare away every half-decent man in East Tennessee."
It wasn't like Lou to feel sorry for herself. Ben knew it was more from the scare he'd just given her than from any weakness in her character. In every fine sense of the phrase, she was truly his big sister, and his proclivity to take a tumble now and then worried her greatly. His tolerance for pain gave her no comfort. To Ben, Lou's anxious concern was the only true hurt his work-related accidents ever caused him.
"Well that's amazing and disheartening all at the same time. Maybe it's because you're a girl, but you've just blown Joe's theory."
"Theory on what?"
"Theory on throwing a baseball."
"Ben honey, can we talk about something else besides throwing a baseball? How about we talk about my houseboat down in the Keys? I figure I've got about six or seven more years. It'll be nice on my boat, in the breeze, high up on the waves. You, Eloise, and Puckett can come down when

Daddy's not visiting. Who knows, maybe the men down there don't scare so easily."

"I'm not talking about throwing a baseball. I'm talking about Pastor Lumpkin."

"Ben honey, come here… no wait let me come over to you." Lou cupped Ben's face, looked into his eyes, and then rubbed his head. "Well, you don't appear to have any dents from that fall. But you aren't making a lick of sense. I really think you should go on to the doctor now."

Another man may have taken offense at being handled like a little boy. But Ben wasn't that type of man. He recognized love, even when it came out clumsy. "Hear me out, Lou. I'm talking about how Pastor Lumpkin throws a baseball. He throws a baseball like a girl."

Lou released his head roughly.

"I mean he throws like most girls. That's not right either. What I'm trying to say is he doesn't know how to throw a baseball."

"So?"

"Well, don't you think that may say something about his upbringing, maybe even his character?"

Lou laughed a giggly laugh. It didn't come out often, but when it did it always reminded Ben that his sister-in-law was, in fact, a woman. "I know," he said. "It's stupid isn't it? You shouldn't judge a man by his arm strength."

"Honey," Lou held her hand to her chest to suppress another embarrassing giggle, "You're as lost as a possum at noon time. And Joe? Shame on Joe. A man of his literary sensibility should have more of a clue about character."

"So you think it doesn't matter?"

"Ben, there's a reason that Jesus hung out with fishermen."

"What does that have to do with anything?"

"With all those high priests meandering about Jerusalem,

why do you suppose that Jesus decided to throw his lot in with the common folks?"
"I don't know."
"Because they could throw a baseball."
"I knew it! I was just afraid you'd grab my head again."
Lou worked hard to keep her giggle soft. "You do know I'm not talking about an actual baseball. I'm talking about what throwing a baseball represents."
"Yes ma'am. I'm following you. It makes a lot of sense. Joe would be proud. How did you get so smart?"
"I've had a lot of time to think. And when I quit work and get my boat, if I can't find a man, and if I don't burn up in the sun, I may just become brilliant."
"So how can it be fixed?"
"What?"
"The baseball problem. You know, the preference for fishermen. It's not good for the folks who are supposed to be leading churches to have such weak arms. You do know I'm not talking about actual weak arms?"
"Yes, honey, I'm following you. And I've got an educational plan. Like I said, I've had lots of time to think. It goes like this: before a preacher follows his call to seminary, he needs to attend Lou's pastoral preparatory academy."
"I'm listening."
"If the young man or young woman hasn't worked in regular life for at least twenty years, they would have to spend a minimum of two years working in the Southwest Virginia coal mines. During that period, they'd be required to get headsplitting drunk a minimum of twelve times and to engage in at least seven knock-down drag-out fights. Notice by the numbers that my plan is all very biblically based. If at the end of that time they can still hear their call, they'd be welcome to go on to the seminary of their choosing. I guarantee you, Ben,

at the end of Lou's pastoral preparatory academy, they'd know how to throw a baseball even if no one ever showed them. And I don't want to speak for The Man, but I'd guess Jesus would be more inclined to break bread with them, too."

"Nobody would do that, Lou. Well, maybe a few but not very many."

"What's your point?"

Ben shook his head slowly as he returned to his work. "You're a smart woman, Lou. How did you get so smart?"

"Thinking, honey. Lots of time to do lots of thinking."

At lunch, Ben called Pastor Lumpkin from the cell phone in his truck. He let the pastor know that he would be honored to head the outreach committee. Pastor Lumpkin seemed pleased, but not surprised. He told Ben to meet him at the church the next day to toss things around. Ben figured he wouldn't need to bring his mitt.

The sun fell down, and darkness crowded the sky. The crew policed the area and then headed to their vehicles. Ben let the other men go and then waved down the new boy's car before it got all the way gone. He leaned in close to the driver's side and spoke softly while the new boy listened. Then reaching through the window of the old Ford Escort, Ben patted the man on the shoulder. Pulling an envelope from his back pocket, he placed it on the dashboard. The new boy's hand emerged from the window, and Ben took it for a long while before letting go. The Escort pulled away slowly, and Ben walked back to his truck. Tripping a little as he went, he half-way crashed into the tailgate.

"You know this is a business don't you, honey?" Lou said obviously looking him over for injuries.

"He's just struggling a little. It'll be all right."

"Good night, honey."

"See you in the morning, Lou."

Unbreakable

In 1993, more than three quarters of a million refugees fled Burundi in the wake of the Ndadaye assassination. Within his mind, Mevin saw them. On the walls of his room in Burkina Faso, he watched them. Frantic beings laden with belongings swelled the paths and roads to Rwanda. But there were four moving against this stream of desperate faces. Two frantically searched for any sign of hope. Two, a little farther ahead, believed that hope had been swallowed by retribution. And once again, Mevin closed his eyes so that he could watch them closer.

ಬಿಬ

Claude argued with Pierre, but not for long. A rage infested the deepest part of Pierre's soul. It made him older than he should have been, more powerful than a boy his age knew how to be. It also made him sick, and sickness spreads.

"You cannot be a coward all your life," he told Claude.

"But, my father…"

"Your father broods in his tent awaiting a miracle. There is no miracle for Burundi. There is only blood. Tutsi blood."

"I will get Mevin to come. It will be better if he will come."

"He will not come. He is without the heart. He does not even know that we must fight. He is much like your father. He believes that prayer will wither the Tutsi. But the time for prayer has passed. Only the machete will wither the Tutsi."

Claude mustered no further argument. Pierre's force of will collapsed him. And while Pierre stole what few provisions were about, Claude reached for the good he could still recognize and took Mevin's Bible. The two walked out of the rain-soaked camp without another word.

※

"Where will we look, Father?" The darkness was deep and Mevin's voice broke hours of silent walking.

"I do not know. I think we will walk until we find them or return to our hill. I do not know. Do you know?"

Mevin could not see his father through the swollen darkness. But the sound of the ragged voice caused the soggy night to seep beneath his skin. His father rarely asked him anything approaching advice. It was a frightening door for Mevin to see open.

"They will look for Hutu rebels," Mevin said, surprised at the clarity of his voice. "Pierre will want to join with rebel soldiers. Pierre will want to kill. And Claude will do as Pierre tells him."

Mevin drew a deep breath, steadying the thoughts behind his words. "We must find the Hutu rebels. It is the only hope we have of finding the boys. Now, though, we must rest. We are very tired and could walk right past them without knowing. It is time to rest. Come, Father. Unfold your blanket and let's move off the road to rest."

In Burundi, children were actively recruited by paramilitary forces on both sides of the conflict. Children required little food and could be disciplined easily. Beatings were regular, and death was threatened to those who fancied running away. Children carried supplies, scouted clearings, and fought. A common practice was to place children at the front of an attack to measure an enemy's strength. Children were told that the best soldiers always met the enemy first. Scatterings of small bodies lay about the country as a tribute to the lie.

The rain gathered strength through the night and soaked whatever dry cotton threads remained in Mevin's blanket. For a time, he watched his father doze fitfully within the thick patch of underbrush where they lay. And when sleep refused to take him, Mevin turned to prayer.

"Lord Father, Jesus Christ, and Holy Spirit be with us this night. Keep watch over us and help us to rest. Be also with Claude and Pierre. Keep them safe through the darkness. When morning comes show us the way to them. Give us guidance to find the soldiers who will surely take them in. Lord, be with Father, especially. Gather his strength. Comfort his sorrow. Amen."

Mevin felt odd about praying for his father in this way. His father demanded no help. His father stood unbreakable. But a change had crept upon Mevin's awareness and settled within his heart. It was not that he somehow awoke to his father's weakness. It was more that he somehow awoke to God's strength. And from this feeling, unknown but oddly familiar, a spiritual assurance called upon Mevin's consciousness with the clarity of an ancient hymn.

ಉಥ

Pierre and Claude found them urinating in a small stream near a makeshift campsite. Standing stock still, the boys anchored themselves out of sight and watched for a while. But Pierre and Claude were seekers and to stay hidden seemed silly. So, emerging from the brush, the boys hailed the small group of rebels.

"Hello," Pierre sounded his deepest voice.

The reaction was immediate. Small arms and machetes appeared from thin air, and one automatic rifle drew a bead.

"No. no," Pierre pleaded, "We are not your enemy. We are Hutu."

There was no guarantee that the motley group was Hutu at all. The Tutsi government was known to encourage the ethnic militias that operated outside direct military jurisdiction. Militia was just a pseudonym for murderers. And without direct jurisdiction, the Tutsi government accepted no responsibility for the actions of these independent Tutsi factions. The practice allowed the government to shrug its shoulders in front of the international community while continuing to pursue an intense policy of genocide. At first sight, a Tutsi militia and a group of Hutu rebels resembled each other more than either would likely care to admit.

"What do you want?" a dark, shiny man from the back of the group asked.

"We want to join you."

Silence gathered the moment, and all heads turned from the boys to the dark, shiny man. "Join us," he spat. "Join us and do what?"

"Kill Tutsi," Pierre whispered.

His copper eyes narrowed, and the dark, shiny man opened his mouth to speak but did not. Then suddenly, forcefully, he laughed. The group of men held their tongues until the dark, shiny man doubled over. Then, the entire group erupted.

Pierre and Claude stood smiling. Still waiting for an answer, they were drawn nearer to the group by the laughter. The dark, shiny man's eyes caught their first steps forward, and the laughter stopped. Striding toward the boys, while other men in the group rolled from his wake, he paused along the way to grab a long machete sticking in the wet earth. Stopping in front of Claude, he brought the machete's blade alongside the boy's neck.

"How about you, silent one? Do you wish to kill Tutsi as well?"

"Yes sir," Claude whimpered.

Taking a step back, the dark, shiny man examined the boys. "We fight for democracy. Democracy in Burundi!"

"Democracy in Burundi!" the group of men shouted.

"You are ours now. You will do as you are told. Go now and collect the men's garments. Wash them in the creek. We will march in one hour."

The boys worked frantically, scrubbing the clothing with a small cake of soap and beating them against the large rocks. The men lounged naked on the creek bank, talking idly and tossing an occasional jeer toward the boys.

There were about two dozen of them, all skinny and hollow-eyed with the exception of the dark, shiny man. The fierceness of his presence openly frightened the group. Their uniforms were not really uniforms at all, more like mismatched hand-me-downs from a parcel delivery service. The chain of command was simple: there was the dark, shiny man, and there was everyone else.

"Hurry your work. We must leave now."

The naked group tiptoed to the creek bank to retrieve their clean, but still wet, clothing. Pierre and Claude wrung out the last few garments and climbed out onto the bank.

"Move!" the dark, shiny man commanded. The group obeyed and without any apparent direction, they fell in line two-by-two with the dark, shiny man taking up the rear and walking alone.

Claude began to look about for his possessions, but Pierre grabbed his arm and brought him into the line. "They have taken our belongings, he whispered. "We are soldiers now. We must share everything to defeat the Tutsi. Do you…" Pierre's question was interrupted by the swift crash of a rifle butt down upon his left cheek. The boy crumbled to his knees. Blood poured freely from above his eye.

"Silence!" the dark, shiny man hissed. "If you cannot remain silent you will die. Now get up and walk."

Pierre staggered to his feet and leaned heavily on Claude. But the boy was a warrior. Not even a whimper escaped his body. With his friend's help he walked, and within a mile, he no longer needed help at all.

༄༅

Mevin and his father found the campsite—a happenstance explainable only by answered prayer. The chance of such fortune was slim, but God had a way of filling out slim. They found the campsite because Mevin prayed and his prayer was answered. For some, that logic would be a little shaky, but to Mevin the explanation was as solid as a brother's faith.

"Here, Father. They have been here." The smell of urine and piles of human feces gave the recent inhabitants away.

"How do you know it is them?"

"I know, Father, because we have found it."

"But it could be any group. It does not mean it is the rebels that Claude and Pierre have joined. It does not mean it is rebels at all."

Mevin looked around for something to solidify his certainty to his father. And there at the edge of the creek was his Bible. "Look Father. Look there. The Bible. It is my Bible. Claude must have taken it from the camp, and now God has used it show us the way."

Mevin's father went to the book and picked it up gingerly. "Yes, Mevin," he said with the clearness that Mevin knew as his father's true voice. "They are near. We will find them first. And then we will retrieve our Claude and our Pierre."

ಬಿಂಜ

The group of rebel soldiers hiked through the day. The rain fell with a fluctuating intensity that challenged the rhythm of the walk and tired the group quickly. Pierre and Claude fought to keep pace. Their eyes stayed focused ahead and away from the dark, shiny man's rifle butt. There was no indication where they were going or why. It seemed only that they must walk and stay quiet. Hunger gnawed with a rawness that caused their bodies to slump. Dizziness titled their strides and threatened to cast the boys to the ground. Night fell before the dark, shiny man called for a halt.

"Here. We will camp here. You," he grunted at Pierre, "take this and prepare it." He handed Pierre a bag of cornmeal. Pierre took it and stood in silence. "What is the matter with you?"

"I…"

The dark, shiny man backhanded Pierre to the dirt. "Silence. How about you, quiet one? Do you know how to prepare a meal?"

Claude did not answer. The dark, shiny man threw up his hands. "Uhh. What good are you two?" Then looking at Claude for a long moment, he abruptly slapped him to the ground beside Pierre.

Without being asked, another man gathered the bag of corn meal and began preparing the group's dinner. The dark, shiny man retired to the brush while Claude and Pierre moved cautiously to the edge of the men's activity. The boys weren't allowed to eat that night, but exhaustion overwhelmed their hunger, and they fell soundly asleep.

ஐౚ

Mevin and his father made good time through the day's rain and by nightfall, they could hear the low voices of men.

"We cannot rush in like an elephant. We must stalk first and wait for our time. To move too soon is to risk death for Claude and Pierre. For awhile, we will follow."

Mevin thanked God for his father's instruction. It cooled his heart like a cloud in the dry season. His father had revived with hope, and it filled Mevin with a deep comfort.

ஐౚ

The rebels traveled through the country's narrow valleys, stopping only at darkness. On the third day of their trek, the dark, shiny man dispatched a pair of his soldiers to round up some food. Within hours the pair returned, well-stocked with provisions either stolen or donated from a village on a nearby hill. That night, Claude and Pierre ate with the group for the first time. The two scavenging rebels also brought word that government soldiers were in the area. And for the next several days, the dark, shiny man led his group in a circular pattern around a series of hills. Eventually, they came upon a small contingent of government soldiers marking time at a military roadblock.

"Here," the dark, shiny man scolded his soldiers, "Stop here."

The rebels watched the contingent of soldiers for several hours. Finally, the dark, shiny man led his group up a portion of a hill that overlooked the small road. "I am ready for the attack, but wary of the ambush," he spoke aloud to no one in particular. "You. Tutsi killer. Go down and take some corn to the soldiers. Offer to sell it to them. See what you can."

Pierre stood and was handed a sack of cornmeal from a hollow-eyed rebel. Pierre looked briefly toward Claude and started back down the hill.

"Tutsi killer," the dark, shiny man whispered. "If you do not return, we will eat the silent one for dinner."

From above, the rebels watched Pierre approach the roadblock. The government soldiers ordered him to halt, but he kept going, claiming that he had items for sale. The government soldiers became visibly agitated and chambered rounds in their weapons. But Pierre continued, insisting that his package was very valuable. As he drew closer and they could better assess his stature, the soldiers lowered their guns.

"What is it you want, boy?" one soldier questioned.

"I have some food to sell."

"Sell?"

The soldiers broke into laughter and one reached forward to snatch Pierre's sack. "Goodbye, boy."

"But there is a price," Pierre persisted.

"Yes boy, there is," a soldier said stepping forward and unsheathing his machete. "And it is your head." Raising the blade above his shoulder he swung at Pierre. Turning quickly, the boy leapt back and ran. The soldiers' laughter followed him into the brush where, without warning, he was pulled hard to the ground.

Pierre could not breathe, and his eyes swelled with shock. The hand covering his mouth clamped tight while he was dragged deep into the brush. The hand relaxed, and Pierre gulped air greedily before turning toward his assailant.

"What?"

"Shhh," Mevin's father commanded. "It is us, Pierre. We have come to get you. You will go with us."

"It is okay, Pierre," Mevin said stepping up beside his father. "You will go with us and it will be okay."

Pierre eyes darted between Mevin and his father. Finally, in a whisper he said, "I cannot."

"You must. You will," Mevin's father told him.

"No. I cannot. If I do not return, they will kill Claude."

Mevin's father sat. And in silence, he stared at Pierre. And then rubbing his head with the palm of his hand asked, "What is it the rebels plan to do?"

"We will attack this roadblock and kill the Tutsi soldiers."

"When?"

"I do not know."

"Then, you will return, and we will wait. When the rebels and the soldiers begin to fight, Mevin and I will come to you and Claude. Be ready. Tell Claude to be ready, too."

It was now Pierre's turn to stare in silence. He looked deep into the eyes of Mevin's father. And then without another word, he climbed back through the brush and up the hill.

"What did you see," the dark, shiny man shook Pierre as if to wrench the information out of him.

"I saw no more soldiers, only those on the road."

"What did you hear?"

"I heard nothing besides the birds."

"Why did it take you so long to return?"

"I am a small boy. My legs do not carry me fast up hills."

The dark, shiny man released Pierre and returned to his watching. "I do not know," he said aloud. "We will wait a little longer."

The rebels lounged, quietly waiting for instruction. The government soldiers below them told jokes and laughed loudly. At dusk, the dark, shiny man turned to his group, "It is time." And the group gathered to a semi-attention.

"You two will go first," he said nodding at Pierre and Claude. "Here," he said handing each of the boys a 9 mm pistol. "It is loaded and ready to fire. Hide your pistols in your pants and go back to the roadblock to sell another sack of corn. When the soldiers command you to stop, fire your guns. Aim at their chests. Do not stop shooting. If there is an ambush, we will know then. If not, we will attack from behind you."

Pierre and Claude crept back down the hill with the dark, shiny man and the rest of the rebels close behind. Before the boys broke from the brush, the dark, shiny man whispered, "It is better to be shot in the front than in the back."

Day was in full retreat by the time the boys walked the road. A light rain fell, making the shapes that could be distinguished blurred and suspect. Before the guards called out for them to halt, the two made it a lot closer to the roadblock than Pierre had earlier.

"You, on the road stop! What is your business?"

"It is I, Sir. I have returned with another sack of cornmeal to sell."

"Go away."

"But, Sir."

"Go away or be killed."

Pierre hesitated briefly, and then stepped forward. A single shot rang out from behind the soldier's roadblock and whizzed between the boys. But while reaching into his pants, Pierre kept moving forward. Claude stood, anchored to the road, not reaching, not moving. The 9 mm came alive in Pierre's hand as he fired wildly toward the roadblock. And without warning, the brush rose up around them. Government soldiers, hidden and unseen from atop the hill rushed up the road toward the dark, shiny man and his rebels. Gunshots filled the air behind, in front, and all around. The 9 mm was spent, and Pierre quit moving—standing in the center of the road, waiting on a bullet. He was hit from the side and knocked hard to the ground. But then quickly, he was up again and being dragged to the opposite side of the road.

ඊඞ

Mevin watched his father dash out and grab Pierre just before he made the same move for Claude. Bursting from the brush, he clambered onto the road and grabbed his brother's wrist as he ran for the other side. Jerking violently, Claude's body gave way as Mevin pulled him along. The 9 mm fell from Claude's pants and bounced along the road, momentarily chasing after them. Reaching the safety of the brush, Mevin found his father, and the two dragged their captives as far from the gunfire as their lungs would allow. Chests heaving, they stopped for a while, but did not speak. And without a word, they stood and ran again until they could run no more.

The night fell deep before they found a place in the brush to rest. Claude cried fiercely, but Pierre remained stoic.

"What now?" he said looking directly at Mevin's father.

"We will return to the camp, then I will send you boys away, away from the camp. I have cousins in Burkina Faso. I will beg of them to help us. You can go there to live for awhile. You can go to school there. After… It is up to God."

Pierre made no response. Turning from the conversation, he fashioned a place on the ground and lay down to sleep.

Exhausted, the others followed suit. When daylight awoke them, Pierre was gone.

Mevin could not comprehend his leaving. Where would he go, back to the killing? Back to a certain death? He turned to his father again.

"Why?" he pleaded.

"I do not know. I cannot tell you." His father's voice turned frail, and he began to sob heavily. "We must go. We cannot go back again. Some embraces are unbreakable. Pierre Ngabo is gone from us forever."

☧

Following the flood back to Rwanda, Mevin's family returned to the camp. This time, there would be no tent. Even plastic sheeting was scarce and commanded a high price. Hope abandoned the camp for good. And after living on its fringes for another year, at the ages of sixteen and twelve, Mevin and Claude left their father for the West African nation of Burkina Faso. He kissed them goodbye and promised to follow as soon as the money and paperwork allowed. Within months of their departure, Rwanda exploded into a seizure of ethnic cleansing. Hutus in the country rose up in a fit of retribution against their Tutsi brothers. When the machete was finally sheathed, close to a million Rwandan Tutsi, along with thousands of Hutu moderates, lay slaughtered. It was another unimaginable number.

On the morning of their first day of school in Burkina Faso, Mevin and Claude learned of their moderate father's murder. They wept together briefly and then attended their classes. The western world never fully appreciated the carnage in Africa. Tears of anguish for people like Mevin's father would never be rightly shed. Songs of praise and honor remained silent and un-composed.

A Different Kind of Sense

Preachers, at least most of the ones that Ben had heard, were fond of saying that life got in the way of God. But many of the folks Ben went to church with, the regular folks, believed it much more likely that God got in the way of life. Such times, they said, were a beautiful inconvenience. So as a consequence, these Godly changes of direction were most often revealed to those who didn't mind taking their faith a little out of the way. Ben didn't really know whether leading an outreach committee was something God wanted him to do or not. But he did know that it was an inconvenience. And it was definitely out of his normal way. He took it as a good sign.

The Outreach Committee met on Thursdays in the old library section of the church. The bookshelves were long gone, so there was plenty of room to slide metal folding chairs across the hardwood floor and congregate in a circle. Ben started the gatherings with prayer. "Dear Lord, guide and direct us. Show us what you want us to do. Help us to reach out and touch your will. Give us the strength to submit. Amen."

Ben had never been the literary type, but he'd written the prayer himself. He'd thought about getting Joe Shelton's help, but in the end decided it was his to do, so he did it himself. He was glad he did. Slow to show pride, it was still more than obvious that Ben was pleased with how it had come out. It especially tickled him the way the prayer played with the word "outreach". The committee seemed to like that too, but the slow nods of their heads indicated an even greater partiality toward the notion of having the "strength to submit". In watching their reactions, it occurred to Ben that the same scrap of writing could be known in a number of fine ways. And that if life was like a melody, the words chosen to fill it were better judged by the reaction they invited than by what you actually meant them to say. It was almost like the words had a life of their own. Ben figured that was probably why Joe liked words so much.

Pastor Lumpkin picked the committee himself. And for the first few meetings, Ben couldn't figure out how he had made the cut. But one night, looking around at the graying smiles of his committee mates, it dawned on him. He was there to do the heavy lifting. And the weight wasn't just figurative in nature. Grocery bags for shut-ins or boxes full of hand-me-down coats wouldn't sit upon the brittle bones of the other committee members. Making Ben chairman assured his attendance at every outreach function. He'd always be there to pick something up. "You are a cunning rascal, Pastor," he said aloud, smiling at one of the nightly meetings. "A cunning, cunning rascal."

"What was that you said, Ben?"

"Oh nothing, Mr. Unsler, I was just working something out in my head."

Mr. Unsler was a Pastor Lumpkin supporter from way back. He'd been on the search committee that had issued the Pastor's call, and he'd lobbied heavy to give Pastor Lumpkin competitive compensation. Ben knew that Mr. Unsler came to keep an eye on things for the pastor, but that didn't bother Ben in the least. He didn't expect to do anything that would even cause Mr. Unsler to blink.

"Well if you're finished, I've got an idea for a new project."

In the first few months of its existence, the First Communion Outreach Committee had done both a canned food drive and a coat drive. It wasn't a bad start, and they were looking for something similar to do next.

"You have the floor, Mr. Unsler. What do you have in mind?"

"Refugees."

"Excuse me?"

"I said refugees. You know, like folks from another country who don't have anywhere to stay. We could help them out. You know, get them started in a new land—the whole American dream and whatnot."

"I don't know, Mr. Unsler," Ben said, looking around to the other committee members for support. "A canned food drive is one thing, but I don't know if we're ready to take on refugees. I'd be afraid that's a little more than we're ready for right now."

"Well, I have a piece of paper from Pastor Lumpkin. It's all about how churches in Chattanooga have been working with this outfit to help settle refugees from Eastern Europe. You know, the old Soviet Union."

"Well, Chattanooga is a bigger place," Ben said, easy so as not to invite an argument. "They most likely have bigger churches with outreach committees that have been together more than a few months. They probably even have paid outreach people who spend all their time just working at the church."

"But this paper is from Pastor Lumpkin. It's from him directly. He gave it to me himself. I think you best have a look at it."

Ben reached for the copy of the newspaper article, just to be polite. *Best have a look at it*, he thought. *Best have a look at it, or what?* He let the thought go before it turned into something he'd rather it not.

Mr. Unsler forced the paper roughly into Ben's hand, and the feeling was immediate. Warmth was how Ben could best describe it. The piece of paper was warm like a heavy cotton towel fresh from the dryer. And there was a softness to it, like it would be nice to hold up to your cheek. The feeling spread through Ben's hand and up into his arm.

"Did you just copy this? It's… it's warm."

"No," Mr. Unsler croaked. "Pastor Lumpkin gave it to me yesterday."

"Well, it's the oddest thing. I get this feeling, it's like…" Ben's words died amid the loud screech of his metal chair begging the hardwood floor for traction. But the two couldn't come to terms, and the chair shot from beneath Ben's backside, sitting him forcefully upon the floor. The chair then titled forward and smacked him spitefully on the back of the head. The old library went dark for a moment, but Ben soon sensed the presence of Miss Emma positioning herself to try out the CPR she'd mastered over at the senior center. The light returned.

"It's okay. I'll be all right in a minute."

"Are you sure?" Miss Emma asked, not quite ready to return the teeth to her mouth.

"Yes ma'am. I am quite sure."

The meeting ended on account of injury and the absence of anything else to say. Ben promised Mr. Unsler that he would read over the article and follow up with the appropriate people. He promised Miss Emma that he was still okay and then climbed in his truck to head home. He was unsuccessful in hiding his injury from Eloise, who strongly advocated a call the doctor and, when Ben refused, made him wear an ice pack on his head throughout dinner. After a no-holds-barred wrestling match with Puckett, a story from the well-worn children's Bible, and a bed-time prayer, he took a bath then lay down next to his wife.

"Did the outreach meeting go all right this evening? I mean other than when the chair attacked you." Eloise laughed softly from the next pillow.

"Very funny. You better be nice. I think Miss Emma is sweet on me. I may just decide to take up with her."

"You could do worse."

"I've already done better."

Ben reached for his wife and felt her warmth, and he remembered the copy of the newspaper article still lying on the passenger-side seat of his truck. He wanted to tell her about it, but he was too tired and sleep crept over him quickly.

༄༅

The height squeezed, forcing Ben's body to tense against the pressure. He hated heights. But Ben was there, out on an open ridge, all by himself. The vastness underfoot collapsed his lungs, and he struggled for each breath. It occurred to him then that he was dreaming. He wouldn't have scrambled up to this rocky altitude of his own conscious accord. But still, it felt real, and the voice that came to him in these situations came now. "Jump," it said. Ben's knees turned milky and the voice came again. "Jump."

While open-eyed, the thought was ridiculous, and it was no less ridiculous now. Ben had no desire to jump, to hurt himself, to end it all. Life found him absurdly happy, but the voice was still compelling. It was oddly powerful. "Jump," it said. The voice was why Ben didn't do well with heights.

He woke briefly, long enough for the relief of it being "just a dream" to seep into his awareness. But he was asleep again quickly, and the dream was back. This time there were two ridges. Within a long hop from where he stood, another collection of shell and limestone rose high above the world. There was a clump of pines on the opposite ridge, and from somewhere in the branches a crow called to him: "Caw. Caw. Caw." Ben had an unnamed aversion to crows. He assumed it had come from his Granny Catherine, but maybe it was farther back than that. It didn't matter. He felt no compulsion to hop across the high empty space between the ridges just to commune with a crow.

But the crow was persistent. Its caw drew him from his paralysis, and he took a shaky step toward the edge. "Jump," the voice hissed. "Jump," it said again with a vengeful intensity. Ben awoke, and he forced himself out of the bed and into the kitchen. A glass of milk was good for washing away bad dreams. And when Ben lay back down, he dreamed no more of heights, and voices, and crows.

༄༅

"What's the matter with you, honey? You're moving around like your boots are full of mud." Lou eyed Ben with a look of concerned disdain. It was a look that only Lou could muster.

"I didn't sleep well last night. I kept dreaming about heights. You know how I feel about heights. And crows, too. There was a crow in my dream. I don't much like them, either." They were doing touch-up work on a small job in Kingsport. The early winter sun stretched hard to move past the trees, and morning still hung early in the air.

"Ben, honey, do you ever ask yourself if you need to do something else?"

"Something else?"

"Something else. Like another job."

"I'm just a little tired. I'll be all right in a minute," he said as a smile lit within his eyes. "You aren't going ride me all day, are you?"

"I'm not riding you. I'm not even talking about the fact that you're working like a preacher on a Monday. I'm talking about the fact that you are a roofer who is accident-prone and afraid of heights. That's just not a healthy recipe, honey. It's just not healthy at all."

"I'm not accident-prone."

Lou gave Ben a long look. "Listen, honey, I know why you do this. I know that my sister and my nephew are the reason you climb high and don't cry when it hurts. And I love you for it. You are the most noble body I've ever known, but you don't have to do this forever. In a few years, I'm going to get my boat and be floating high down in The Keys. All I'm saying is you ought to think about what you might want to do next."

"Lou, has God ever talked to you?"

"You haven't listened to anything I've said have you?"

"Yes I have. I'm supposed to think about what to do next, because I fall off roofs a lot and don't particularly like being up on them in the first place. But that's not what we're talking about now. Try to keep up." Ben's smile spread from his eyes to his face. "The question on the shingle now is, has God ever talked to you?"

Lou settled into one of her looks, but Ben rode it out and waited for an answer.

"Yes, honey. I suppose He has."

"Tell me about it."

"If I tell you, you're not going to like it much. Might bring back some things you've decided to forget."

"I'll be all right. I'd like to hear."

"It was about the thing with you and Daddy. Do you still want to hear?"

೨೦೦೮

Ben's marriage to Eloise was not without trouble. They had been high school sweethearts and Ben had always gotten along fairly well with Eloise's daddy, Bob Grainger. In fact, at sixteen, Ben started working for Mr. Grainger's roofing company. Bob Grainger had no sons, and Ben had no father. It seemed to fit well. Folks said how nice it was that things tend to work out the way they are supposed to. In spite of his occasional accidents, Bob Grainger told those same folks that Ben was one of his finest workers, almost as good as his older daughter, Lou. That was high praise from a man of Bob Grainger's caliber, for he was not only one of the finest roofers in the region, but also the deacon of First Communion Church. Bob Grainger's wife was always sickly, and she'd died early in their marriage. With two young girls to raise on his own, Bob Grainger had turned hard to the Lord. He was a staunchly moral man who drew rigid lines. Folks respected him for it. There was no better person to have on your side, and none tougher to stand against you.

One bright early morning, Eloise had walked into Bob Grainger's kitchen, pregnant. Ben was beside her as she told the deacon the news.

"Whore!" he thundered. "You filthy, ungrateful whore!" He raised his hand, but Ben caught it on the way down. The two men struggled. The strength pitted in that kitchen was more than most dare challenge. But, finally, Ben gained the advantage and shoved the deacon across the table and onto the floor.

"Just let us leave," Ben had said evenly. "All we want to do is leave." He helped Eloise squeeze past the table and turn toward the door.

Picking himself up, Deacon Grainger grabbed a kitchen knife that had fallen in the ruckus. He charged Ben's back and plunged the blade between his neck and left shoulder blade. Ben wheeled quickly and with a strong right hand broke the deacon's jaw in two places.

The fight was over and Ben and Eloise climbed into Ben's truck. Eloise was crying desperately and begging him to go to the Emergency Room, but Ben told her, "I'll be all right. I just need to get to Joe Shelton's house and I'll be all right." He drove Eloise to his house first before going to see Joe. When he got there, the steak knife was still sticking in his back.

"You've got to get yourself to the hospital. This is a job for a doctor," Joe told him.

"No. I don't want to see a doctor. I don't want to bring trouble to the deacon. I need you to take it out for me."

"Boy, you're going to send me back to the bottle."

Joe had found more than one good reason to quit drinking, but at that moment he sort of wished he hadn't. "I need you to hold still. I'm going to try and do this quick."

Joe eased the knife out, trying not to widen the wound. As soon as the tip cleared the skin, blood gushed like a swollen creek. They hurried into the bathroom, and Joe pressed cold wet towels on the Ben's back. Gradually, the bleeding stopped, and Joe bandaged him the best he could. Then he excused himself, went outside, and threw-up on the back porch. Joe didn't much mind the sight of blood, but such a quantity… He supposed things were different in quantity.

"Different in quantity," Joe thought as he went back inside. "I might be able to fashion something Country and Western out of that."

When Joe opened the door, he found Ben busy cleaning his bathroom.

"What are you doing?" he asked.

"I've made a mess. A person ought to clean up his mess."

Feeling the smile spread across his face, Joe looked at his friend. "Ben, you make a different kind of sense."

Ben smiled back. "Now that sounds like a line in a country music song. You ought to write that one down."

From that time on, Deacon Grainger never spoke a word to Ben or Eloise. And Ben and Eloise lived with the silence. Sunday after Sunday, they attended the same church service with no acknowledgment from the man who used to love them. Puckett's birth changed nothing. The little boy knew that the man in the far pew was his grandfather, but he had no concept what the word "grandfather" was supposed to mean. It might as well have been "stranger". A blasphemy walked into the sanctuary and sat down upon the back pew of First Communion Church. It wasn't the only one taking up space back there, but this one resided in its most harmful incarnation—a failure to forgive.

☙❧

Ben shifted his weight and teetered on the edge of losing his balance. "Yes, Lou, I still want to hear."

"Okay. Well, I know it was hard on you and Eloise to have Daddy shut down on you like he's done. It breaks my heart, especially for Puckett. But you got to know that I love Daddy. He's hard, and it hurts everybody around him. But he's my Daddy, and I can't help but love him."

"Eloise can't either."

"I know, honey. And I've prayed for his heart to melt. And I've prayed about what I should do. And do you know what God told me? He told me to do nothing. He told me to wait. Can you imagine that? I'm terrible at doing nothing. I'd rather hurry and do something that's wrong than wait to do something that's right. That's partly how I know it was God that told me to do nothing. He's got a way of working through a weakness."

"How?"

"How does He work through a weakness? Come on Ben, honey, don't you ever read your Bible?"

"No. I mean how did He talk to you?"

Lou laid the nail gun down and sat on a small dormer overlooking the front yard. "Well, honey, it's not going to make any sense, so it's tough to explain. It's not like some big bearded face looked down from the sky and said, 'Hey Lou why don't you try doing nothing for a while? That's right I said nothing.' It was more of a feeling that came upon me. No, that's not right, it wasn't a feeling. It was more of a knowing. That's a better word for it. It was a knowing. I'd been praying and thinking about what to do about all that mess, and one day I was just riding along in my truck, and it came over me. I knew with a certainty that I needed to just hold my horses and wait. I tell you, honey, I didn't like the notion one iota. But that didn't matter much, because I knew that it was God answering me. It was God. I just knew.

"You and I had already started the process of striking out on our own with the roofing business. I never could get God to answer me on whether I should keep going that way or not, but I saw no reason to change. Daddy was about ready to retire, anyway. So here we are sitting on this roof. And here I am still waiting on the Lord."

"Thanks for telling me, Lou."

"You're welcome, honey."

"Lou?"

"Yes, honey."

"I think God might be trying to talk to me. Something happened at church last night, and then I had that crazy dream."

"I thought something like that might be going on."

"The thing is, I'm afraid that He may be talking to the wrong guy. I mean, if I'm reading this right, it seems like I'm being led to look into helping some refugees come to America. I've hardly been out of Hawkins County. I'm the last one in the world anyone would ask to help some refugees."

"Honey, that's the surest sign that it's Him who's asking."

"You're no help at all, Lou. I'm thinking it was the tendonitis in my arm acting up last night that caused it to be so warm. And it was that bump on the head that caused my crazy dream. That makes a lot more sense than it being God."

"Have you prayed about it?"

"No. And I don't plan to."

Lou laughed her surprisingly giggly laugh. "Ain't none of my concern, Ben honey. It's between you and God. But my money's not on you."

Ben turned and caught the toe of his boot on an upturned shingle. He stumbled awkwardly toward the roof's edge before being steadied by Lou's firm grasp.

"Thanks," Ben said, righting himself. "That one might've hurt."

At lunch, Ben prayed in his truck. It wasn't the kind of praying he'd settled into. It was different somehow, less practiced, more honest. "Lord," he said, "about this refugee thing, I really don't want to have anything to do with it. As a matter of fact, it's silly that I'm asking you about it, because you probably weren't even trying to talk to me about it in the first place. But if you were, Lord, I'm listening. At least I'm trying to. Help me to know, Lord. Help me to know."

Ben opened his eyes and caught sight of the copy of the newspaper article still lying on the passenger-side seat, and he knew. He found his cell phone and dialed the number on the bottom of the page. A nice lady answered and listened to him for a while before giving him a different number to call. He called it, and another nice lady from Bridge Refugee Services in Bristol answered the phone. She was overjoyed to hear from him. It turned out that there was a fairly immediate need for resettlement help in the Tri-Cities area. She told Ben he was the answer to a prayer.

"What part of Eastern Europe are these folks from?" Ben asked.

"Eastern Europe? What made you think they were from Eastern Europe? Land sakes, Mr. Bellamy," the lady seemed on the verge of laughter, "These gentlemen are about as far from Eastern Europe as you can get."

Original Purpose

There would be no refugee camp in Burkina Faso. Mevin and Claude lived together in a small, bare apartment. Their relatives left them to their own devices, even entrusting them to manage the modest sum of money they gave the boys on behalf of their father. Days consisted of school, basketball, and worship with a small Anglican community of fellow refugees. They ate one meal a day; money was better spent on tuition and books. Mevin and Claude lacked the necessary papers to secure regular work, but they made some spare change by running errands or taking the occasional odd job. Life was safe but uncertain. Burkina Faso had not adopted the Geneva Refugee Convention, and the government was under no obligation, political or otherwise, to harbor refugees of any sort. A bureaucratic decision was all that stood between lives of relative security and returning to the horror they had fled. With no work and no true home, Mevin and Claude waited, educated themselves and prayed.

Mevin, of course, also stared at the walls, but Claude would be back soon. So, Mevin said the words he always said when the time for staring ended. "Lord God, Jesus Christ, Holy Spirit," he whispered, "Give us the will to wait. Let us not be disheartened. Help us to find our home."

After the prayer, Mevin gave in to a smile. He couldn't help himself. Inside his head, he could hear his father's voice caution that a prayer was not always answered the way it seemed. But, his prayer had been answered. How exactly? Well, that would wait for later. But the very fact that it had been asked and answered was a reason to smile. And Mevin knew that his father would understand. His father was no doubt smiling, too. Mevin could almost see it. On the wall, he could almost see his father's smile. It was the painting he'd been looking for. It was the window he'd been seeking.

Mevin thought of Claude and his smile grew wider. For six years, he'd been waiting to tell his brother this news. Mevin had practiced it. In his mind, he had spoken words of hope and of future. Now, it was time to do so for real. Now, it was time to speak them aloud and to hear them with his own ears.

The United Nations High Commission on Refugees grew nervous about the shaky situation in Burkina Faso and began petitioning the United States, as well as Western European nations, to accept refugees living in that country. The U.S. embassy in Burkina Faso conducted interviews with each and every refugee with the desire to pursue life in America. Another series of interviews followed, and two years after they had entered the process, Mevin and Claude were approved for resettlement by the Immigration and Naturalization Service (INS) of the United States of America. Mevin had received word while Claude was in class.

"We are going to America, Claude," Mevin leapt toward his brother as he opened the door to the dwelling. "We have grown up without a home, but now we can grow old as Americans." The words came out differently than Mevin had practiced them, but they were still good words. They were the best words.

"Will we see Michael Jordan?" Claude asked.

"It is a big country. I do not know where he lives. But maybe. It is, after all, America."

The INS handed Mevin's and Claude's case off to World Migration Ministries, who, in turn, worked with several agencies, including Bridge Refugee Services. Placements into communities were made more or less at random. Success rates and current case loads were factored in, but mostly it was simply a matter left to the grace of God.

ಬಿಂಬ

"You sold any of cows yet, boy?"

"Not lately."

"Your cows are getting some age on them. What do you plan on doing when they start dying off? Don't want to spend all your time just digging cow holes."

"I suppose I'll cross that bridge when I come to it. How about you? You written any new songs, Old Man?"

"Not lately."

"Your songs are getting some age on them. What do you plan on doing when the royalties peter out? Can't spend all your time just figuring on the next good song."

"I guess I'll cross that bridge when I come to it, too."

The morning came late and crisp. The oaks still held stubbornly to a smattering of red and yellow, but the black walnut trees stood bare like naked old men. There at the gate, an early piece of winter stood with Joe and Ben. And it didn't take a pair of reading glasses to see the whole of it coming down the road.

"What's the matter with you Ben? You're fidgeting like a dog without his flea collar," Joe said, thinking that Ben clearly had something on his mind.

"I've got something on my mind, Joe. Something I'd like to speak with you about."

"Go on then."

"What do you think about bringing a couple of African refugees to Mt. Carmel?"

"What for?"

"I don't know. So that they can start a new life, get away from war and hunger and that sort of stuff."

Joe thought on the subject for a bit. "Africans in Appalachia," He pondered out loud, "Now there's a scrap of alliteration that would fit nicely in a song. Trouble is I'm not sure which kind, because nobody would believe such a thing."

"I know. It sounds crazy. And I don't have time for that kind of craziness. I need to make sure that I'm always around for Puckett. The most important thing to me, at this point and time, is to be a good father. I can worry about Africans after Puckett grows up."

Ben drew a deep breath as if to take an account of his own rambling. They stood silently in the cool morning air, waiting for more words to come. Ben took off his hat and then put it back on. He kicked at the grass and shifted his weight from left foot to right and then back again. He just couldn't stand still. After a while, Joe felt the need to speak.

"You're about to come out of your britches, boy. You can't stand still and that's not like you. It's apparent to me that in spite of what you say, you're wrestling a mighty powerful urge to invite some Africans to Mt. Carmel. What in the world has gotten in to you?"

"Has God ever talked to you before, Joe?"

"I haven't always been a good listener. Most likely over the years, He's tried."

"Well, I think He's trying to talk to me right now. I keep having this crazy dream about being up on some high ridge and seeing a crow. And every time I go to pick up a copy of a newspaper article, I get this warm feeling. But it's not even all that. It's just that I know it's what I'm supposed to do. It makes no sense, but I just know God wants me to do it."

Joe didn't have the faintest notion what Ben was talking about, but he didn't tell him that. What he said was, "Well, boy, if you know that's what God wants you to do then the question you need to ask is what's keeping you from doing it."

Ben rocked back on his boot heels. Joe thought for a minute that he might take another tumble, but Ben righted himself and looked long at some early rising clouds. "I don't know, Joe. I don't know what's keeping me, but it's not going to keep me anymore. We're going to bring some Africans to Appalachia. You better get started on that song."

Ben said his good-byes and almost skipped back down to his barn. Joe stood watching and couldn't help but give in to a small shake of his head. "Lord," he said. "If it is you talking to Ben, please speak clearly. And if you aren't the one in his ear, please get there soon."

༄༅

Mevin and Claude waited four weeks for space on a plane. World Migration Ministries looked for the best possible airline deals. The better the price, the more refugees they could afford to fly. So when good deals came available, they took them, and when there were no good deals, they waited.

Mevin and Claude didn't get much notice before receiving their final flight arrangements. They were in class when word reached them. They took a few minutes to say farewells to friends, teachers and fellow students before heading quickly to their small apartment. Gathering clothes, photographs, and Mevin's Bible into a couple of makeshift carry-on bags, they were in and out in less than half an hour. There wasn't much to take, and there was no call for deep nostalgic sighs. It occurred to Mevin that without such things, good-byes grow short. He rubbed his hand along one of the walls and then closed the door on them all.

The plane lurched and bumped its way to Paris. Having never flown, Mevin assumed that air travel was always this rugged. But sensing the anxiety of his fellow passengers and watching the flight attendants become ever more shaken, he considered the fact that something might actually be wrong. He reflected briefly of the irony of dying in flight, but caught sight of his frightened brother and brushed the thought aside.

"Do not be afraid, Claude. God will not let us die here. We are going to America. America holds a purpose for us. We will not die. Believe, Claude. You must believe."

The hard landing in France left them breathless. But they had made it to solid ground, and they thanked God. The eighteen-hour layover made them too fatigued to be frightened, and they boarded their next flight willingly. The atmosphere over the North Atlantic was passive with only mild bouts of turbulence. They made New York City feeling better about their chances of living. Eight hours later, they boarded a plane to Atlanta. The first flight from Atlanta to Tri-Cities regional airport was overbooked. The second was cancelled, so they spent the night in Hartsfield International Airport with plans to take the first flight the next morning. Mevin and Claude didn't know enough to be upset over the delays. With smiles and nods, they listened to the rapid English spoken over the loudspeakers by the constantly-explaining airline representatives. Other would-be passengers stomped around and carried on like it was the end of the world, but Mevin and Claude had spent most of their lives at the center of some sort of wait. This by far was the easiest one.

ഌ

The First Communion Outreach Committee was plain fired-up.

"Way to go, Ben. Pastor Lumpkin will be so proud," Mr. Unsler beamed. "What do we do now?"

Ben was prepared for the question. Bridge Refugee Services provided him with all the literature necessary to help settle a refugee in East Tennessee. Step-by-step paperwork laid out what paths needed blazing and which mountains would most likely have to be climbed.

"We need to get some volunteers to head up some teams for medical, language, housing, legal residency and other stuff.

But first we need to take a vote on whether the Outreach Committee wants to commit First Communion to doing this project."

"Why, of course we do," Mr. Unsler boomed.

"Well, let's just talk about it a little bit first. The refugees that are next on the list are from Burundi."

"Is that in the old Soviet Union?" Mr. Unsler asked.

"No. No it's not. It's in Africa."

"Africa?"

"Yes. Africa."

The group fell silent as they pondered the change in geography. "What are their names?" Miss Emma finally asked.

"There are two brothers. They lost their mother and father in the fighting between some tribes over there in Africa. Their names are Mevin and Claude."

"Are they Christian gentlemen?" Miss Emma prodded.

"Yes ma'am, the best I can tell. The information I was given says that they grew up in the Anglican Church."

Quiet gathered within the old library again. Ben waited long for some kind of indication from the group. Though his whole being ached to speak, to plead, to explain that this was not something that could be voted against like a new zoning ordinance, he kept his own countenance. Something stronger than himself told him to wait, not to force, not to cajole, just to wait, to wait on the Spirit.

"Well, I can't see as how where they are from changes a thing." Mr. Unsler was smiling. "I'd rather have someone named Mevin and Claude anyway. I could never pronounce those Eastern European sounding names worth a darn. Too many consonants, not enough vowels."

"Call for a vote, Ben," Miss Emma suggested.

The vote was unanimous, and the old library buzzed with an audible fervor not permitted as part of its original purpose.

Ben assigned committee members to teams and told the group that he would give the final word to the nice lady at Bridge Refugee Services.

"Tomorrow, I'll also give Pastor Lumpkin a holler, let him know where we came out on our vote, and ask him for some time in front of the congregation. I'd like to get the whole church involved."

"Ask them to pray for us, Ben," Miss Emma said. "Involvement is good, but what we really need is prayer. Don't forget that."

"Yes ma'am. I won't forget."

Ben promised to call each member of the committee as soon as he heard anything about possible arrival dates. Team leaders would begin their work immediately and check back in with Ben to get coordinated. Ben resigned himself to a high cell phone bill and knew the effort would be like herding cats, but he didn't care. All he cared about was doing this thing, because he knew it was the thing he was supposed to do.

※

Ben's cell phone rang. Usually, Lou wouldn't let him carry it up on the roof for fear he would get distracted and fall off in mid-conversation. But Ben insisted that he needed to be constantly reachable and promised that he would be extra careful.

"Don't even think about it, honey," Lou warned.

"What? We talked about this. I've got to have it up here."

"I know. But don't even think about answering that thing until you back off the edge and go sit down next to the ridge vent."

Smiling broadly, Ben reached for the phone on his belt.

"Don't you dare, Ben honey. Don't you dare."

Ben didn't dare. He ambled toward the center of the roof and punched the button on his cell phone after its sixth or seventh ring.

"Hello."

"Who is this?" The caller demanded.

"Who is this? Ben responded.

"Is this Ben Bellamy?"

"Yes, it is."

"Son, I need to see you in my office right this minute."

"Who is this?"

"Don't try and be funny, son. I'm in no mood for foolishness. Meet me at the church."

"Is that you, Pastor Lumpkin?"

The phone went dead, and Ben stood up, but only for a moment. Losing his balance, he plopped down upon some newly laid roofing felt and slid feet first past Lou and up over the gutter. It would have been a pretty fancy dismount if his back belt loop hadn't caught hold of a window sill. The unexpected tug pulled him back and then pitched him forward. He lost his center gravity and was unable to keep from landing face-first into a large rhododendron.

"Don't come down. I'll be all right in a minute," Ben yelled almost before he landed. "Stay up there. I'm all right." He continued stepping from the bush and spreading his arms wide so that Lou could inspect him.

The whole crew peered down from the rooftop, poised to climb down the ladder, but there was nothing in obvious need of repair.

"Are you sure you're all right, honey? I can call a doctor."

"No. I'm fine. And that had nothing to do with the cell phone, nothing at all. I'd already finished talking. I'd already hung up."

"Okay, honey. Whatever you say. Just as long as you're okay."

"I'm okay. But I've got to run by the church for a while. I'll be back before lunch. And since I'm laying out for a while, I'll buy."

The crew gave a muted hurrah. The promise of a free lunch always generated enthusiasm. Ben piled into his truck and steered it toward Mt. Carmel.

☙☕

First Communion looked more like a small castle than a church. Large weathered stones piled atop one another and gave the square building a solid, lived-in look. A short bell tower jutted from the roof and an iron cross stood watch over it. Red doors, an aesthetic borrowed from the Episcopalians, shared attention with the grays of rock and mortar. The structure elicited a feeling of permanence, a sensation of resilience.

Ben crossed through the sanctuary. Its morning quiet eased him deeply. There was just something about a silent church, almost like it was resting. Passing through the kitchen area and into the back offices, Ben found the church secretary away from her desk. So he knocked on the large oak door with the engraved brass plate that read, "Pastor Lumpkin".

"Enter," a smooth voice called.

In contrast to the structure housing it, the office was modern. It bordered on being plush with its large glass-covered desk and chairs made of steel and leather. But the crosses cast about in various places atop shelves and on walls provided just a hint of humility. So, plush would not have been an appropriate description, overdone was perhaps better. Framed photographs outnumbered the crosses and crowded every eye-level space upon the four walls. Large men in robes shook hands with the pastor and peered piously at the camera. Smiling politicians in seersucker suits patted him upon the back. Minor celebrities embraced him and sealed the encounter by signing their pictures with practiced hands.

Each time Ben entered these chambers, he searched among the frames for the image that would put him at peace with all the other clutter. It became harder for him to find with each visit. Ben wasn't quite sure whether it was because Pastor Lumpkin's clutter had increased or his ability to see around it had diminished, but with a sense of relief his eyes finally lit upon the photograph of the pastor's family. A little dated, the picture revealed a rather somber crowd. The pastor's plump, round-eyed wife sat in a winged-back chair with two stick-thin male adolescents and a rather rotund but pretty-faced girl kneeling around her. The pastor stood behind them all, looking slightly toward heaven. Ben found the poses a bit on the formal side; still, it was a nice portrait—a nice family portrait. The pastor's children were grown and rarely visited. Ben had met them all but the older boy one Easter, shortly after Pastor Lumpkin arrived at First Communion. He was trying to recall their names when the pastor interrupted his effort.

"Son, we've got a problem."

"A problem?"

"Yes a problem. A big problem. I got a call from a lady at a place called Bridge Refugee Services this morning thanking me for our church's willingness to help some African refugees."

"Oh. I'm sorry about that. I'd planned on calling you at lunch to tell you about the Outreach Committee's vote. I guess she beat me to the punch."

"Well, I've been trying to get in touch with Unsler all morning. He won't call me back. So, I had to call you. Tell me, Ben, what in the world is the Outreach Committee thinking?"

"Excuse me?"

"Don't be coy with me, son. You know what I'm talking about. These refugees are from Africa. There's a good chance that they're black."

Ben viewed the pastor. He seemed big in the pulpit. But behind the large, glass-covered desk, he looked bloated and small. His soft manicured hands rubbed the steel rails of his leather chair as he waited for Ben to speak. His hair, sprayed into submission, did not move with the rest of his nervous body, and small beads of sweat stayed perpetually anchored to the top of his red forehead. For the first time, Ben really knew that this pastor was no fisherman. Oh, he had suspected before, the way he threw a baseball being Ben's biggest clue. But as much as he hated to admit it to himself, now he truly knew. This man made his living from God instead of for God. Ben decided right then and there not to take any more of his crap.

"Well don't just stand there leering at me," the pastor bellowed. "What do you have to say for yourself?"

"Do you have a problem with them being black?" Ben asked.

"Oh no, not me. It's not me that I'm worried about here. It's the congregation. This is the type of thing that could split a congregation. And we don't need that do we? In Chattanooga, they have had a lot of success with Eastern Europeans. We want success here, Ben. Now why don't you just call the woman from this Bridge place back and politely decline the Africans. I'm sure someone else will take them. We'll wait. The right refugees for us will come along in God's time." The pastor grew calm as he spoke. His mouth seemed to soothe his soul, the sound of his own voice lifting his spirit. "You can use my phone. Go ahead, give her a call."

"I'm not going to do that, Pastor," Ben said matter-of-factly. "Nope, I don't believe I'll be making that call."

"What?"

"I said, I'm not going to call the lady back and tell her to find someone else to take the Africans."

"Ben, be reasonable."

"Is there anything else you wanted to talk to me about? I need to get back to work."

"Listen. And hear me clearly on this. I will not have… Africans coming in and sending my church into a tizzy."

"Your church?"

"Don't get sanctimonious with me, you foul product of sin. You unwanted life. You bastard." The pastor gathered his full brimstone voice. "From a fetid beginning you came and from a fetid beginning you continue. You sit in the pew not even talking to your wife's father, smearing your child in the stain of your own life, in the shame of your own disobedience. And then, you come in here and think you can preach to me, think that you have any say in how this church will conduct its business."

Ben didn't respond. He held the pastor in a silent gaze and waited. The quiet again infected the pastor with nerves. And finally, he just seemed to have to speak. "Ben, my son," he said now in his getting-ready-for-prayer-time voice. "We are both upset. But in the end we both know it would be wrong for us to bring Africans into this congregation. Look at this," he said pointing to his note pad. "One's last name is Ntwari. The other is Kamenya. They have different last names. They must have different fathers. Their mother probably had many men. You know how these kinds of people are. Their faith is not like ours. They have different experiences. Christianity probably means something entirely different to these people—something a whole lot less. They don't depend on their faith like we do. You don't want Puckett influenced by people like that, do you?"

Anger found itself foreign in Ben's heart. He just hardly ever got mad. Nonetheless, it seemed odd to him now that he harbored no rage. He pondered his own calm briefly before speaking. "Pastor, where are you from?"

"Excuse me."

"Where are you from? Where did you grow up?"

"That's a strange question to be asking right now. But I was a preacher's son, so we had the benefit of moving a lot… Northern Virginia, Florida, Massachusetts, California. I guess you could say I grew up in a lot of different places. Why do you ask?"

"Just checking an assumption."

"And what assumption would that be."

"That you're not from around here."

"No. No. I'm not from around here," the pastor laughed softly. "But now I'm curious, what gave rise to that assumption?"

"Well, I'll tell you. I've spent my entire life somewhere within a hundred miles of Mt. Carmel. So, I don't know a lot about people from other places, but I do know the people from this part of East Tennessee fairly well. And in the whole time I've been living amongst these folks, whether I am or not, not one them has ever called me a bastard."

"Ben…"

"Let me finish pastor. I've got a couple of things left to say." Ben leaned forward like a prizefighter, and it may have been his imposing physical stature that shut the pastor up. But the pastor had to know of Ben's kind countenance, and that the chances of Ben actually deciding to harm him were slim. So it must have been something more that caused the pastor to find the silence he so desperately fought. "Pastor Lumpkin, you underestimate your congregation. You have no idea how good the people who fill this church really are. Maybe, you don't even understand that it's those same peoples' faith and not the walls, or bells, or even your sermons that make this God's house. I hope to God that you have some inkling of what I'm trying to say. But as far as it concerns the Africans, it doesn't really matter. Come next Sunday, I'm going to stand up during announcements and tell the congregation what the

Outreach Committee has decided. What God has decided."

A tremor ran through the pastor's body. His entire being began to shake. "God? What God has decided? Who do you think you are, speaking to me about the will of God?"

"Just a man, Pastor. But come Sunday morning, I'll be a part of something that's a whole lot bigger than that."

"You're confused about the way things work."

"I think I've got it figured pretty well."

"You wouldn't dare stand up without my consent on this."

"I wouldn't bet on that, Pastor. You can't ever tell what a bastard's going to do."

Ben was done talking, a natural result of there being nothing left to say. He gave a nod to the Pastor and silently excused himself. The Pastor half-yelled something as Ben strode down the hall, but it wasn't loud enough to hear. Or maybe, it just wasn't worth listening to.

Awkward Grace

Joe stood alone at the gate. Ben had already gone to work, but sometimes after he was done puttering around in his barn, Joe would limp back out and linger alone for awhile. Most times, he would think of Catherine Bellamy. He missed her greatly. And somehow standing there between his place and hers, he missed her less. He wished he'd been enough to make her stay; to decide that life still needed living. But once Ben hit high school, Catherine had faded quickly. Her work was done. The reason for living was no longer strong enough to subdue her grief. So, she'd passed. And Joe was left with only memories and wishes. But there were worse things, Joe thought. His memories made him laugh and there at the gate he could almost touch his wishes. He wondered if the same was true of Ben's Africans. What memories kept them company? What wishes dare they try and touch? Joe decided that he didn't really have it so bad, and his thoughts kept after the Africans. When and if they came, what would they be thinking? How would they even get from Africa to Mount Carmel? "Airplanes of course," Joe said to himself, "A whole lot of airplanes."

Whenever Joe flew on an airplane, he always felt like he was going to die. It didn't keep him from flying, though. In fact, he sort of looked on it as a good thing. It wasn't that he wanted to die. He was always hoping for a few more good years. It was just that it caused him to take stock of his life whenever he felt like he was facing death—kind of put things in order. Whatever forgiveness was left locked up, Joe tried to set loose, and whatever importance found harbor within his ego suddenly seemed hilarious. It was not such a bad thing, flying on a plane and preparing to die. So, Joe supposed that flying on a plane and preparing to live must be beyond wonderful. And as he turned from the gate, he couldn't help but figure that there had to be the makings of a gospel song in there somewhere.

❧☙

His face pressed tight against the window, Mevin took in the changing topography below. Beside him, Claude slept, but Mevin couldn't. The morning sky woke bright and cloudless, and the small commuter plane climbed to only a modest altitude. The land lay visible to anyone with the curiosity to peek, and the foothills surrounding Atlanta gave way to the bright green of the pine-covered North Georgia Appalachians. On into Western North Carolina, the pines maintained their stand, but the closer the plane drew to East Tennessee, the denser the hardwoods became. The effect was subtle, but the green of pines and pasture changed. The gray of leafless hardwoods crept into the color, casting a deeper hue. And gradually, a darker green covered the hills and valleys and seemed to place itself into the whole of existence.

Small geometric plots added depth to the landscape; even in winter evidence of the people's aversion to anything fallow. Mevin smiled through the window. He liked this place from above, not that it mattered. This would be home, whether he cared for it or not. In the end, he knew he would find a fondness simply because it was home. But it was a fine experience nonetheless to feel as though he might like it just because of what it was. It was nice to think that, given a choice, he may choose for himself this dark green land instead of it being chosen for him.

"Claude, awake. We are approaching the airport. We are meeting our people. We must not look asleep when we land."

❧☙

It bothered Ben greatly, but he passed Pal's restaurant anyway. He told himself that his promise would not go unfulfilled, only delayed. Lunch was important to a work day, and a late lunch could cloud an effort as sure as an afternoon thunderstorm.

"I'll buy them all milkshakes, too. They'll not appreciate me being late, but a Pal's milkshake will make it easier to take. A Pal's milkshake can cure almost anything." Ben spoke to himself above the crooning on the country music station. He spoke aloud now to reassure himself of his ability to do so later.

The house sat small and simple, and Ben's Ford filled up the width of the gravel driveway. A green, weedless yard lay evenly before a structure of brick and whitewashed wood. Some hardy pansies still lined the pine-mulch flower beds, and large groupings of winter greenery lay serenely under leafless maple trees. The whole landscape looked like it had just been swept.

"Neat as a pin," Ben told himself, "Neat as a pin."

The truth had a way of coming at a man from strange angles, and despite their self-centered slant, some of Pastor Lumpkin's words rang with it. And, through all the other noises, Ben heard it clearly. To say he was nervous would be inaccurate, but his hand shook as he raised it to knock. He pulled it back and rubbed on it for awhile. Uncertain was what he felt, and though uncertain could look a lot like nervous, in Ben it came from a much deeper place. He raised his hand again and pushed through the uncertainty. Three solid raps brought a quick answer. The oak door opened, and Ben's father-in-law stood square-shouldered before him.

He was on in years, but the Deacon was still a powerfully built man. Ben took him in a moment before speaking. "Mr. Grainger, it's time to move on. Past time, I'd say. Eloise, Puckett, and me would like you in our lives. I'd appreciate you getting to know Puckett. He's a good boy. He'd benefit greatly from your grandfathering. Anyway, I'm hoping you'll reconsider the way things are."

The Deacon filled the doorway in silence. Ben lingered just a moment, then turned from the door, walked to his truck, and drove to Pal's.

ಬಿಂಕ

"Morning, Joe," the usher said as he extended a program for the order of services.

"Good morning, old buddy," Joe responded because he couldn't remember the man's true name. "Looks like, we've got a crowd today."

"Yep. But I think there are some seats near the front."

Joe nodded his thanks and then headed toward the back.

Pews weren't usually hard to come by at First Communion, but that particular Sunday was an exception. Folks piled in close together, most likely hoping that their neighbor's perfume was applied in moderation. The sermon sounded a call to obedience. The language was general in nature, and as usual spoke nothing too specific with regard to the First Communion congregation or the region of East Tennessee. Joe had the growing suspicion that Pastor Lumpkin just pulled his sermons out of some paint-by-numbers homily handbook. And neither good song nor good sermon had ever been written that way. Near the end, though, Pastor Lumpkin made a point aimed squarely at Ben.

"The church is a body. And just like a body we can't give in to urges, even ones that seem to feel good at the time, which will cause the body as a whole to suffer. Obedience and its interpretation is where we should seek direction. And I, as the spiritual leader of this church, am willing and able to help discern that direction. I have spent time at seminary, brothers and sisters. I have devoted my career to the Lord. I am willing and able to discern that direction."

Time for announcements came, and Ben walked down to the communion rail without even being asked. When he turned back toward the congregation, his face was aglow.

"I have some great news. The Outreach Committee has voted to sponsor some refugees from Africa. Now this means a lot of things…"

"When was this vote taken?" The voice from the pulpit seemed to surprise even the elderly organist who'd seen just about everything four walls and a cross could offer. Pastor Lumpkin usually ignored the announcements completely, busying himself while they were read. It was quietly understood that laity took the lead during this portion of the service. His intrusion seemed to sit ill with the entire congregation.

As for Ben's part, he remained serene, looking as if he'd just tasted his first spoonful of sourwood honey. "Why Pastor, you know when the vote was taken. You and I talked about that very subject earlier this week."

"That we did, Ben. That we did. But subsequently, I also had another conversation with a member of the Outreach Committee. Mr. Unsler, would you please stand up."

Mr. Unsler rose slowly. Eyes downcast and darting, the poor man's shirttail escaped from his belt and hung loosely from his waist. "Now Ben," Pastor Lumpkin continued, "Was Mr. Unsler at this Outreach Committee meeting?"

Ben's glow had not dimmed one iota. "Yes sir. And we were glad to have him there."

"Mr. Unsler," the Pastor said with obvious relish, "Was there a vote in the affirmative for sponsoring refugees from Africa?"

Mr. Unsler paused as the church creaked and popped its silence. "I don't remember."

The answer seemed to startle the Pastor a little, almost like it was less than he had anticipated. But the broad smile that crept across his face also indicated that he thought it was still more than enough.

"Brothers and sisters, there seems to be some confusion about this matter. I'd suggest that we call for a time of discernment; some needed time to decipher God's will. I'd be happy to lead this effort."

A feeling swept through the church. Even in song, Joe had always found it tough to describe communal feelings. They weren't solid to the touch and yet they were still as real as a rock. So, from the back pew Joe struggled with his compulsion to surround this feeling with the right words. In the end, he decided just to call it an uneasy feeling, a feeling not unlike the recognition of evil. The congregation soaked in it a while, and the good people shifted and stretched in their pews trying to shake it loose. The whole church went to squirming like children at a fine restaurant. Joe felt for Ben as he stood there, still smiling like a baboon. This thing Ben wanted to do, this thing he thought God told him to do, was being wrestled from him by a smooth talking, world-wise preacher. Joe began composing a song of lost opportunity in his head. But admittedly, Joe should have known God better than that.

"There doesn't seem to be any confusion to me." Joe watched the broad-shouldered man stand as he spoke. Neatly dressed, the crease in his pants could've cut hay. Joe's eyes told him who it was, but belief hadn't quite convinced the rest of him. So, Joe listened hard as the broad-shouldered man continued. "Ben seems to know what happened, and Mr. Unsler doesn't. Seems pretty clear that we ought to hear from Ben about what we need to do for these Africans."

"I remember now," Mr. Unsler's voice broke as he shouted, "I remember, we did vote, and it did pass. There's no confusion now. No confusion whatsoever."

"Well," the Pastor offered.

"Well," the broad-shouldered man answered.

The two stood locked in an old fashioned stare-down, but not for long. Under his striking church robes, the pastor was soft. He couldn't stand the weight of such a public disagreement. But the broad-shoulders of Deacon Grainger were more than up to it.

"Alrighty then," the pastor said, casting his eyes toward the choir. "Let's hear what our outreach chairman has to say."

Ben tore a puzzled gaze from the body of his father-in-law, and the goofy look took hold of his face again. He stepped toward the congregation and promptly stumbled into the parishioners on the front pew. "Oh I'm sorry," he told the ladies with white purses. "I lost my balance. I think my foot has fallen asleep. I'm truly sorry." Righting himself, he moved toward the center of the church, among the congregation, and began to speak.

"Within the next couple of weeks, we will welcome refugees from Africa to our church here in Mt. Carmel, Tennessee. Only God could think up such a thing, and I believe that God's hand is in this. I believe it with all my heart and soul. The members of the Outreach Committee will be contacting you to ask for help in certain areas. If you can help, thank you. If for whatever reason you can't help, that's okay, but whether you can or can't, please pray that First Communion will serve these refugees in a way that will make God smile. Please pray for us to do our best. Please pray for our friends from Africa to do their best. The Outreach Committee will keep you updated. Thank you for your help and for your prayers."

The church buzzed with side conversations, and Joe couldn't tell whether it was from excitement or shock. But as he watched Ben amble back to his pew on a sleepy foot, he came to a belief. From the Spirit present in that church and from the purity of one man's intentions, Joe believed, as much as he had ever believed anything, that no matter what missteps or stumbles lay upon this path, it was the right path. And because of that, everything would work out just fine.

༄༅

On a clear Saturday morning, Ben invited Joe to travel along with him, Eloise, and Puckett to the Tri-Cities Regional airport for the purpose of welcoming two African refugees to East Tennessee. By the time they made the short drive up Interstate 81, it seemed that they had traveled a world away. In the airport, there were actual Africans, and to Joe it seemed like there were a whole lot of them. Of course, he had no idea that such people even existed in East Tennessee so maybe the delight in seeing them amplified their numbers in his mind. The crowd dressed themselves in colors. Robes and hats were on display. Ebony skinned women spoke in rapid, exotic dialects to their friends. Dark angular men smiled broadly at passersby. The first word that awoke in Joe's mind was beauty. The people were absolutely beautiful, almost royal in appearance. Refugees, every last one of them, congregated to welcome their own to a new place.

Joe found a corner and watched. Ben wandered around nodding and smiling. People came to him, shaking his hand and speaking an English sweetened with a molasses accent. Joe knew little about the history of Hutu and Tutsi. And he wasn't sure which kind was gathered here, but he thought it might be both kinds. That sort of thing was possible here. This was a place where your kind was measured more by your output than your ethnicity. It was a better way to pick a kind. The thought of it made Joe a little misty, and he started to sniffle.

"Are you fixing to cry?" Ben ambled up beside him.

"No, I'm not fixing to cry. What kind of talk is that?"

"Well, your face is all scrunched up and your eyes are glassy, it just looks like you're fixing to cry."

"I'm not fixing to cry. I'm just overcome a little. This whole thing is beautiful. It's just beautiful. I'm telling you, it would…"

"Make a good song."

"You're darn right."

"Well, you better get your guitar tuned, because our guys are getting off the plane right now."

Joe opened his mouth to speak, but the words were not ready yet. So, he just looked on in silence at Ben. Ben smiled broadly and put his arm over Joe's shoulders, and the words found themselves.

"You've done good, boy," Joe said. "Whatever else happens, you've done good."

Ben looked to the ground and shook his foot. "I wish I knew why my foot kept falling asleep." Then he let go another broad smile and said, "Thanks. Thanks for saying that, Joe."

Mr. Unsler was beside himself with excitement. Joe feared the poor man may wet his pants. He hollered for Ben to join him at the front of the crowd. The African contingent took up the call, and Ben meandered through obvious reluctance to join Mr. Unsler front and center.

The whole thing was too wondrous for Joe to take alone. He just couldn't help himself, and he turned to a tall African woman beside him and latched onto her for all he was worth. She raised a delighted yelp, and they cried all over each other while they waited on their arrivals.

෴

The plane popped down quickly. Open gates at Tri-Cities Regional Airport were always available, so passengers were stepping onto the tarmac within minutes. Mevin set foot upon the ground and considered his own impassiveness. His heart held neither apprehension nor joy. He felt as if he were walking in mud, unable to fully sense the way he should. "Dear Lord, Jesus, and Holy Spirit," he prayed urgently. "Let me feel. Shake my numbness."

Mevin and Claude followed the line of passengers through the gate and into the terminal. Visitors waited for their travelers in a common reception room, and the more experienced travelers immediately headed in the right direction. Knowing nothing else to do, Mevin and Claude followed along, hoping to be recognized.

Claude saw the crowd first and gasped. "Mevin, look!"

Mevin heard before he saw. Salutations in French and Kirundi called them past the security checkpoint and up the long hall. Shouts of joy echoed off the tiled walls and left the two no choice but to smile. The sounds nudged Mevin's heart toward responsiveness, but the sight of a large, pale man, hands folded quietly in front of his body, shook loose in Mevin an elation he considered long dead. A goodness oozed from the pale man, a goodness that flowed to those around him like water to a dusty garden. Mevin thought, "This is a man who is close to God. This is the man who has brought us here."

ଽଠଷ

From across the excited throng, Joe watched as Ben and the one they called Mevin, approached one another. Seeming to be unfamiliar with how to extend a proper greeting, they stopped together and simply nodded. And they stood there just looking at one another, not knowing what to do and not being able to say anything that the other would understand. It was a little awkward, Joe thought, but it was also somehow the most joyous thing he had ever witnessed. What were the words for it, Joe wondered. How could words ever describe such a thing? And then without warning, the words came. And for the first time in a very long time, he wrote the words down. Stepping away from his embrace with the tall African woman and reaching deep into a pocket of his dungarees, he fished out an old grocery store receipt, found a pen on nearby counter and scribbled the words, "awkward grace".

And then, from somewhere near heaven, the awkward grace shook completely loose and descended upon the waiting area at the Tri-Cities Regional Airport. Mevin extended his hand, and Ben took it with both of his. But within that awkwardness was even more grace, and when the tears started rolling down Mevin's face Ben took hold of him and hugged him with all that he had.

Puckett ran to his father and was enfolded within the hugging. And soon, the one they called Claude joined in. Then came Eloise and Mr. Unsler and after them the entire Outreach Committee. The bunch of them stood there amongst shouts of praise and joy from the crowd just holding on to one another like it was the only thing they were ever meant to do.

Joe pushed the receipt back into his pocket and bathed in the glory of it all. He was a regular church-goer, had attended some good revivals, even seen Billy Graham, but there in Tri-Cities Regional Airport was the holiest place Joe had ever been.

Giving Thanks

After the welcome at the airport, Mevin and Claude spent the next couple of weeks at Ben's farm. Before the plane touched down, Ben had stayed outwardly confident in his two years of high school French. But, like a deer caught in headlights, his linguistic skills froze tight at the airport and they never seemed to recover. So, Mevin, Claude, and Ben came to the understanding that it would be better for them to move closer to English than Ben to French. Mevin worked especially hard and in a matter of days he was piecing together rudimentary sentences.

Joe visited often and watched as Puckett stared at the Africans for long periods of time while Eloise fed them large quantities of unfamiliar food. Mevin smiled through it all. The Bellamy's surrounded both Claude and Mevin with their bustling warmth and made the whole of creation seem as simple as one family's love.

During those weeks, Mevin woke early each morning and walked to the gate with Ben.

"Joe this morning?" Mevin would invariably ask along the way.

"Yes. Just like yesterday," Ben would respond, smiling.

"Sold any cows, Boy?" Joe said as soon as they reached the fence.

"Not lately."

"Written any songs, Old Man?"

"Not lately."

Mevin stood quietly listening for meaning amongst unfamiliar words.

"We found an apartment down near the church. Mevin and Claude are moving in on Saturday," Ben said, finding a stream of conversation to follow.

"That's good. A man needs his own home," Joe answered, glad that a conversation was afloat.

"It's not much."

"Doesn't need to be."

"We could use an extra truck to haul the furniture we've collected."

"I'll meet you at the church first thing Saturday morning."

"There is one more thing we could use."

"Name it."

"Until these fellas get their driver's licenses, they're going to need some transportation. I'll pick Mevin up for work, but they're still going to need someone to take them to the grocery store, the laundry mat, and…"

"Out on dates."

"Yes sir. That kind of stuff. I hate to ask you."

"Ben, I need you to understand something. When I'm able to help you, it makes me feel better than I have a right to."

"Thanks, Joe."

The silence sat ill at ease. Sudden intimacy was hard to recover from. Mevin looked closely at Ben then at Joe, "Sell a cow. Write a song. Let us go to work."

The laughter flowed honest and brought them back to solid footing.

"You're all right, Mevin," Joe said. "You're a good man." And Joe was right.

&ೞ೦ಽ

In the grand scheme of things, six months was not a long time, and there was almost nothing that could happen that would matter much in the grand scheme. But Ben knew he lived more small than grand, and in the small scheme of things, a lot could change in six months. And six months later a lot of things had.

"You're as crazy as you look, Lou," Ben chided.

"Well, honey, all we have to do is get down off this roof and run a sanity check."

"So let me understand this. You're saying that I can choose anyone on this roof as my partner, and you'll take what's left and still beat me in basketball."

"That's what I'm saying."

"You do realize that there is a very tall black man on the roof."

"I see no black man."

"What are you talking about?"

"I see no black man. That's what I'm talking about. All I see is three pale faces and an African."

Ben snuck a quick peek at Mevin. He was listening to the exchange with a look of bemusement. After six months, Mevin's English was good enough to catch more than just the gist of the rapid but low-key challenges. And after five months on the roof, Ben figured Mevin knew Lou and himself well enough to fully comprehend their competitive affection.

"Lou, you've bit off more than you can chew. Your winning streak ends today."

"Okay then, honey. We'll play at lunch. I've got a basketball in my truck. And these folks have a nice place to shoot. Pick your partner, Ben."

"Hmm. I choose Mevin Ntwari."

Mevin looked up and smiled at the mention of his name.

"Okay. I choose Stumpy Samples."

Stumpy, a short, stocky man with thick forearms, dropped his head to his chest. Stumpy was prone to sneak a smoke or two during lunch breaks and there was little doubt he rather do that than try and anticipate one of Lou's passes. "Are you sure about that Lou?" he asked in weak protest. "Daryl over there played basketball in high school, and he's got me by six inches."

"Yeah, honey, you're my guy. Don't worry, we'll beat them quick. You'll still have time for that lunch smoke."

The crew worked through the rising heat of the morning. Even though they had not really needed another hand, Lou hadn't fought Ben over Mevin's hiring. It was a good thing. Mevin picked up the craft quickly, and he worked... well, he worked like a refugee with no other option. With Mevin's help it wouldn't be long before they could split crews and take on more business. Lou was reluctant to grow. She told Ben it only set her deeper in a life she found shallow. But Ben was close to convincing her that the extra money would get her to a boat on the Keys that much sooner.

"Playing to ten by ones. You got to win by two. Ladies first." Lou fired the ball at Ben. "Check."

Ben held the ball. "Okay, Mevin, you guard Stumpy. Understand?"

"Yes. I understand."

Ben pushed a soft bounce pass back to his sister-in-law to complete the check. Stumpy cut to the basket, and Lou hit him chest-high with a no-look pass. Driving quickly, the stocky man rolled in an easy lay-up with a surprisingly smooth touch. Mevin had not moved.

"One to nothing," Lou giggled.

"Mevin," Ben said smiling. "What happened?"

"Very quick," Mevin responded.

Ben laughed deeply. "Yes very quick," he said putting an arm around his partner. "Maybe we ought to drop into a zone. You know zone?"

"Yes, I know zone."

"Okay, our ball. You take it out, Mevin."

"Very good." Bouncing the ball to Lou, Mevin said, "Check."

Firing it back, Lou responded in kind, "Check."

Ben cut to the basket, but stepped on an errant shoelace and crashed heavily into the side of the garage. Mevin froze with concern while Lou stole the ball and hit Stumpy under the basket for another easy lay-up.

"You all right, honey."

"Yeah, I'll be all right in a minute."

"Good. Because it's 2-0, and I'd hate for you to miss out on your coming humiliation."

Straightening himself up off the concrete, Ben looked at Mevin and said, "We're in trouble."

"Come," Mevin motioned to Ben.

Ben walked over, and the two spoke in whispers.

"This is too quick. I can not move and dribble this quick, but I can shoot. I learned this in Burkina Faso. I can shoot very well."

"Okay. Here's what we'll do then. You pass it to me. And I'll stand right in front of you so that you can shoot."

"Very good."

"Very good."

"Check," Mevin called, tossing the ball to Lou with a little more force.

"Check," Lou responded, a smile sneaking across her face.

Throwing a two foot pass to Ben, Mevin stayed put while Ben dribbled right back to him and handed the ball off. Ben's big body shielded Lou from any steal attempt and Mevin launched a shot. Striking high up on the backboard the ball found the front of the rim and rattled home.

"Great shot! Now we're in business," Ben whooped.

Lou's smile bloomed fully, "I guess the bank is open, honey"

Defensively, the game didn't go well for the all-male team. Ben kept falling all over the driveway, and Mevin mostly stood stock-still, transfixed by Lou's assortment of passes. But they still kept it reasonably close. Lou and Stumpy couldn't get around Ben to pressure Mevin and bank-shot after bank-shot rattled home.

In the end, though, Lou and Stumpy won easily. "Not bad Mevin," Lou said on her way to put the ball back in her truck. "If not for you, honey, y'all would have no points at all."

Stumpy went to catch a smoke while Ben and Mevin sat down to their lunch coolers and the daily language lesson. Mevin said grace over the meals, and Ben asked his usual question.

"Got any words today?"

"Yes. What is this, honey?"

"Honey?"

"Yes. Honey."

"Well. Honey is made by bees. Buzz, bees, you know. It is very sweet like syrup. Do you understand?"

Mevin's confusion shone upon his face.

"Buzz. Bees. You know insects. They make honey in their hives. It is very sweet."

"Yes, yes, I know this. Bees make honey. It is *miel*. Very sweet. Very good."

"Good. Another new word. You got any more?"

Mevin concentrated silently on his sandwich. Typically, he'd have a dozen new words to go over every day.

"What's the matter, Mevin?" Ben asked.

"Why does she call me this?"

"Call you what?"

"Honey."

"Who are we talking about?"

"Lou."

"Oh."

"What does this mean? That I am made by bees."

Ben laughed through his baloney and white bread. "What do you want it to mean?"

Mevin was struck dumb by the question. But Ben suspected that it was less because he didn't understand its meaning and more because he was embarrassed about its answer. Ben admitted to being slow in affairs of the heart, but even he picked up on the skittish affection that had flown in and perched itself upon the roof. And it wasn't just Mevin either. Aside from the times she held a basketball in her hand, Lou would not look the man in the eye, and she rarely addressed him directly. Ben thought that he'd smelled some perfume and he'd swear that Lou's cheeks were rosy with make-up. But maybe she just started washing her face better. Ben knew not to ask. He valued his life more than his curiosity.

"I think you're blushing, Mevin."

"Blushing?"

"Never mind," Ben said putting his arm over Mevin's shoulders.

"So?"

"So."

"Why am I honey?"

"Honey is a term of affection, but not necessarily real affection. I mean any waitress in East Tennessee will call you honey when she brings your biscuits and gravy. It's like a friendly hello, nothing else. Does that make sense?"

"Yes. Very good sense." Mevin was visibly relieved and though Ben expected the opposite reaction, it struck him as funny. He began to laugh again. Mevin joined him, and two could not control themselves enough to finish their lunches.

Roofing was hot, tiring work, not like the coal mines, but tough enough to tire the body to the point of affecting the mind. Long days left a person numb, and thinking came slowly to the tuckered-out. Even though Ben offered, Mevin would not let Claude work the roofs. He would not let Claude work at all.

"You will go to school," he'd told his little brother. "I will work, and you will become educated."

To Ben, it seemed that Claude wasn't strong enough to resist his brother's selflessness. And within three months of stepping off the plane, Claude passed the GED and was now taking classes at Northeast State Community College. With language classes, Claude's English blossomed as did his ability to comprehend instruction in other subjects. Claude was bright and putting his mind upon his brother's back, he began to excel. His teachers encouraged him to continue his studies, and Mevin puffed with pride at the mention of Claude Kamenya.

ಬಿಸಿ

Joe liked people. He'd met some questionable ones, but overall Joe believed that most folks had enough of God in them to be truly good deep down. But in all his days, he'd never seen First Communion so good. The whole congregation embraced Mevin and Claude like a fat toddler's mama. Food and furniture piled up. Doctors' visits were coordinated. And genuine affection poured free and honest. Of course, it didn't hurt that Mevin and Claude had a willing smile and an appreciation that mingled with amazement. Plus, the two men were just plain good-looking. Joe knew that was an odd thing for one man to think about another man, but it was factual, nonetheless. Strong jaw lines, broad shoulders, and dark, smooth skin cast an almost noble glow upon the casual observer; it was hard not to sit and stare at them. In America, people were all mixed like mutts, and there was nothing at all wrong with mutts, but Joe figured that folks got so used to seeing them that they sometimes forgot what a purebred looked like. Mevin and Claude were purebred, and the wonderful oddness of it drew folks to them.

When Mevin and Claude had moved into the small apartment in downtown Mt. Carmel, the refrigerator overflowed with food. Furniture positioned itself around the place in proper order, and it almost matched. Payments on the phone, electricity, and rent stood paid in full for the first month. The folks at First Communion rallied around Mevin's and Claude's needs in the best kind fashion, but Joe knew that most in the congregation prayed with calloused hands. First Communion folks were hard workers. They'd learned to swim by being thrown in the river, and most held the conviction that help became a hindrance when it was taken unneeded. So after the initial flurry of help, when First Communion folks felt like their new friends had enough for a fair start, Mevin and Claude were on their own.

Joe worried a little about their chances. Honestly, Joe worried mostly for Ben. He didn't have the money to give Mevin and Claude if they needed it. And while the pastor had kept silent since the day Deacon Grainger had stared him down, if Mevin and Claude needed more help from the church than originally planned, it would give the pastor the opportunity to humiliate Ben from the pulpit. But Joe had found that in life, at least in a good life, it was always best to trade worry for faith.

"Mr. Shelton," Mevin caught Joe lightly by the arm after church. "I need your help, please."

"Sure Mevin. Anything." Joe reached in his coat to retrieve his wallet, but Mevin's reach was quicker.

Pulling a crumpled advertisement from a glossy newspaper insert, he handed it to Joe and said, "Is this of high quality?"

The picture showed a 14-carat gold bracelet from a local jewelry shop. The ad claimed a fifty percent mark down, but it was still $105. "It looks good to me, Mevin. Have you got yourself a girlfriend? Do you know the word 'girlfriend'?"

"Yes I know girlfriend, but I have none. This is for Eloise. It is her birthday this week."

"Ben's Eloise?"

"Yes."

"Lord, I forgot. I need to get her something, too."

"Yes."

Joe looked at the picture again. "This is too expensive of a gift. You shouldn't spend that much. Have you talked to Ben about it?"

Mevin looked at Joe for a long while before speaking. Joe thought he might be working through a translation, matching unfamiliar words with their proper meaning. "No. Ben would not allow such a purchase," Mevin said finally. "That is why I have come to you."

"Well, I'm no expert, but it looks like a fine piece of jewelry to me."

"Good."

"Mevin," Joe said as Mevin turned to go. "Let me give you some money to help buy that present."

Once again Mevin eyed Joe for a good long while, but this time Joe got the feeling he'd had no trouble with the translation. "Thank you, but this would not be correct. If it is a present from me, I must purchase it. My work must pay for it. Such gifts are the best reason for work"

"Fair enough," Joe said and then watched Mevin almost skip away with excitement.

Joe rubbed hard at his eyes to try and keep from embarrassing himself again, because it dawned on him then that Burundian refugees had a lot in common with folks from southern Appalachia. With despair as an ancestry, a chance at some kind of self-reliance was a godsend. Hard work was not a burden. It was just a way of giving thanks.

Goodness, Joe thought, *There has to be a song in there somewhere.*

You Can't Ever Tell

Ben once heard, or maybe read somewhere, that finding true love had more to do with proximity than it did with anything else. More plainly spoken, if someone didn't live close by, you didn't stand much of a chance of ringing the wedding bells with them. There wasn't much romantic about that reality, but it made sense to Ben, and he was fairly certain it was not just limited to the marrying kind of love. Folks needed to hang around one another to see if a fondness took root. Staying far away may have allowed for some sort of peace, but never anything as deep as love. So Ben supposed that in coming together, there was a risk that folks would lose their peace in their search for love. But if it happened to work out, they just may fill their hearts with both. That was probably why folks were willing to chance a walk down an uncertain path. And that's what he figured Eloise was doing now.

She fidgeted. Picking at her apron and straightening silverware, Eloise wore her nervousness plain. And though he would never allow it, Ben felt a little jittery, too. After several Sundays of cordial words over juice and cookies following the service, Bob Grainger was coming to dinner. The man's hat had never hung at the home his daughter had made for her family. His grandbaby grew into a little boy without so much as a fishing trip or even a fishing story. The man stayed put in his tidy house away from the mess that made life authentic. Ben didn't like the price exacted on his family by his father-in-law. It was too high and it hurt the ones he loved most too much. But he supposed the whole estrangement must have hurt Deacon Grainger in some form or fashion as well. And Ben knew that coming to visit wasn't easy for his father-in-law and that a man who is willing to do something hard has at least the makings of a good man. Besides, Ben was the one who had asked the deacon to try. And if the deacon was willing to try, it was only right for Ben to try, too.

Eloise invited Lou. The idea was that it'd kind of soften things if Lou was there. Lou declined. It was not Lou's nature to soften things. She said she thought it better for the evening to stand on its own legs.

Eloise made her Daddy's favorite chicken casserole and topped it off with some peach cobbler and ice cream. The conversation started small and formal, then grew into uncomfortable. But at least, on that night the deacon had sense enough not to correct Puckett's slips in grammar or comment on the impropriety of eating black-eyed peas with your fingers. He even smiled at Puckett's endless questions of Ben and obvious affection for Eloise. The evening ended early and left everyone worn out. First steps were tough, and it was bound to take awhile before everyone found their balance. In the meantime all were truly careful to watch their footfalls. And so the visit was much more of a careful walk than a joyous dance. Still on that night, the evening did find its own legs. And so, there was at least a little better place for everyone to stand.

"I'm going on to bed," Ben told Eloise after they had put the last dish away.

"It's only 8:30."

"I know, but I'm about to fall out—must be the cobbler and ice cream. Besides, my foot has been asleep for two hours, the rest of my body must need to catch up."

Ben kissed Eloise and hobbled down the hall. "Ben," she called after him.

"Yes ma'am."

"Thank you."

"There's no need."

"Just take a 'thank you' every now and again. Thank you."

"Why you are welcome, young lady. You are truly welcome."

ങ്കരു

"Mevin, there's something I've been wondering."

Ben and Mevin sat under a tree on Linville Street, eating baloney and white bread sandwiches. Located near the center of Kingsport, Linville lined itself with ancient trees and well-attended yards. It was sort of a fairytale street in a fairytale neighborhood known as Fair Acres. And that's what it was, a neighborhood. Complete with sidewalks and houses with architecture as unique as the families dwelling within them, Fair Acres was indeed a neighborhood, not a cookie-cutter subdivision. Of course, the houses were all at least fifty years old and small by modern-day standards. And, it'd be safe to lay money that the basements were leaky and roofs in need of repair, for which Ben was thankful. But Ben figured if he ever moved from the farm, it would be to Fair Acres. A true neighborhood would be a good place to finish Puckett's raising.

"What is your wondering?" Mevin asked.

After eight months, Mevin's English grew past the rudimentary nature of Ben's vocabulary lessons. Language was more than just the meaning of words, and Ben wasn't much on suitable verb tense or the proper use of reflexive pronouns. So to learn right, Ben suggested outside help, and Mevin took a language class at the local high school on Thursday nights. To help quicken his learning, his teacher encouraged him to watch a lot television, which Mevin did reluctantly.

Ben's limitations didn't keep Mevin from asking him questions. In trying to explain the nature of things in East Tennessee, Ben had once told Mevin, "A man's understanding of things isn't always indicated by his ability to properly express himself. Give a stuttering old hillbilly a hard listen and you may find he has the wisdom of the world clothed in tattered flannel. You may also find he's just trying to talk you out of your last nickel. The point is, you can't ever tell."

But it was obvious that Mevin could tell with Ben. And questions about life and culture flowed from him like a broken water main. For Ben's part, he found his friend to be almost holy with understanding. And in return for his answers, he took the liberty of seeking some of his own. So the two men exchanged wonderings daily. And over baloney and white bread, a friendship awoke that only poets and old westerns seemed to understand.

"I've been wondering about your last name," Ben said.

"My last name?"

"Yeah, your last name. Ntwari."

"Oh. It means courageous fighter."

"Courageous fighter, huh. I can see that. But that's not what I was wondering. Claude's last name is Kamenya?"

"Yes. It means one who is small, but has large intelligence."

"I can see that, too, but that's not what I'm after. You and Claude had the same father, right?"

"Yes." Mevin's eyes shone joyous at the mention of his father. Ben took in his reaction and let it lie for awhile. But after a moment or two, curiosity pressed him on.

"You had the same mother also?"

"Yes." The eyes filled with a distance, a protective distance that caught Ben a little off guard. He moved on.

"So where did you and Claude get your last names?"

"Our father."

"I don't understand. Your names are different. How could they come from the same father?"

"It is our culture."

"What is your culture?"

"For the father to give his children a last name."

"Then how come you don't have the same last name?"

Ben's and Mevin's wonderings were prone to hit rough patches. Understanding often veered onto rugged roads. But honest hearts and patience usually smoothed most any bump or pothole they encountered.

"Okay, my name is Ben Bellamy. Hold on, I'm a bad example, because I ended up taking my mother's name. Let's take Puckett instead. I'm Puckett's father, and my last name is Bellamy. So, when Puckett was born, his last name was Bellamy, too."

"I understand," Mevin said nodding.

"Well, I don't," Ben replied.

They burst out laughing and tried not to choke on their white-bread. Mevin took a long pull of his Dr. Pepper, then began speaking in his soft molasses tone.

"In Burundi, when a child is born, it is cause for great joy. Fathers cannot contain their own excitement. To honor the occasion, in addition to the first name, the father will give the child another name—a special name. Maybe it will be something to do with the weather or the hill on which the family lives. Perhaps it will be tribal or a statement of the current political situation. It is different for every child. Not like your name at all."

"So how do you know your relations?"

"What do you mean?"

"Well how do you keep from marrying your first cousin who you have never met? Without the same last name, how do you know who is in your family?"

"We just know."

"How?" Ben said breaking into a wide grin.

"Communities are very small, and everyone knows who you are... who your father is. We do not need the last name, because we are known. Like God knows us."

Ben leaned his body back and thought about the sentiment. "I suppose God doesn't require a last name to know that He's your father, does he? It sounds nice, Mevin. It sounds really nice."

"It was very nice."

The two finished the sandwiches and started in on the oatmeal and raisin cookies. Even after eight months, Eloise insisted on making Mevin's lunch, which suited Ben just fine. She couldn't very well give her husband a lunch to take to another man without making one for him, too.

"I was wondering something, also," Mevin said, folding the plastic sandwich bag neatly and returning it to the cooler that served as his lunch box.

"Shoot." Ben encouraged.

"Do you not always pray?"

Ben felt distress crease the edges of his face, and Mevin leaned forward as if to take his question back. But no question had ever been taken back before, and Mevin leaned back again seeming to believe that it would be a bad habit to start.

"What do you mean?" Ben asked.

"You do not pray before we eat lunch or before we start the workday. But you pray in church. And I have eaten with you in your home and you do pray before you eat dinner with your family. I hope this question does not offend you."

Ben leaned his body forward. "The question does not offend me, Mevin. And if it did, it would be my own fault. The answer is that I don't always pray. And speaking of it makes me ashamed."

"I don't understand."

"Don't understand what?"

"How you can have so much without talking to God."

"Now, I don't understand."

"The Bible says, 'Ask and you shall receive.' You have rarely asked, but you have received much. Many blessings have settled upon you. How is this possible?"

Ben sat silent and thought about the death of his mother and the abandonment of his father. He always quietly figured that he'd had more than his fair share of heartache. But then he paused and looked at his friend. Despair was this man's bedmate. He'd lost almost everything. And still Mevin believed. Ben wasn't sure he could do it. If he had been through what Mevin had, he figured his faith for dead. Ben did believe. He did have faith. But he also had Eloise and Puckett. He had the farm, his business, and Lou. And he had this dark-skinned man as a friend. He had no reason not to believe. Maybe that was the reason he did not always pray.

Ben looked long into the silence and then into his friend's eyes. He figured that Mevin was worried, thinking perhaps that he'd stirred more than he had intended with this particular wondering. "I think this is a good wondering," Ben said, breaking the silence.

"I am sorry, but I do as well. This land runs over with blessing. Yet, the more I learn of its language, and the more I watch of its television, the more confused I become over God's favoritism for it." Then stopping and gathering a bit of a twinkle in his eye, Mevin continued, "God must be a woman, because He makes no sense to a man."

Ben laughed hard at the suddenness of the humor. "Oh my goodness, Mevin. I wish Joe Shelton were here, he would…"

"Think it a fine topic for a song," Mevin interrupted, finishing Ben's thought.

Ben smiled broadly, before his countenance settled back upon the seriousness of the wondering. "I don't know how it's possible that I have so much, Mevin. I want for very little, so I guess I don't pray very much. That's not the right way to go about it, is it?"

"It is not for me to say, Ben."

"Oh yes it is. If you are my friend, it's exactly for you to say."

"Very well. I will say it then. It is not the right way to go about it."

Ben gave into another broad smile. "I'm going to change that. Even if all I do is count my blessings, I'm going to make sure I do always pray."

"Very good."

"I have prayed some, you know." Ben told Mevin.

"I am sure."

"No, I mean besides at church and supper when Eloise is around."

"When did you do this?"

"When First Communion was deciding to help you and Claude start a new life. I asked, and I received. I prayed, and my prayers were heard."

Now Mevin let go of a grin. "You are mistaken, my friend. It was my prayers that were heard. It is not you who made the prayer. It is you who made the answer."

The baloney and white bread sandwiches survived only in crumbs, and the wonderings found a natural resting place for the day. But Ben found trouble letting it go. He still wondered something, almost painfully, and he felt a certainty around Mevin's ability to soothe it. "Hold up just a minute, Mevin. I have something else I'd like to ask you."

Mevin had moved to stand, but now settled again. "Very good. Please ask."

"If you are able, please tell me about your father."

"I am able. What is it that you would like to know?"

"Was he a good father?"

The light in Mevin's eyes shone again, and his whole body seemed to bathe in the question. "Yes," he said in a whisper. "He was a very good father."

"What made him good?" Ben asked, matching the low volume of his friend's voice.

Mevin directed his eyes, full of light, toward Ben and smiled. "This is not your true question. But that is no problem, for your true question and this one have the same answer. My father filled his life with steadfast love for Claude and me, very much like you fill your life for Puckett. He was a good father, and you are very much like him. I think you have asked a good question. I hope now you will believe the good answer."

"Saddle-up, gentlemen," Lou yelled from the tailgate of her truck, "Daylight's burning."

"Lou sounds very much like the actor John Wayne on the late movies," Mevin said softly as though breaking from a peaceful trance.

Ben laughed lightly, struggling back from a peace of his own. "She acts like the Duke also." Watching Lou slide off the tailgate, Ben turned to watch Mevin watching the same thing. Turning back, he caught the tail end of Lou looking back to watch Mevin. Hmm, he thought, "You can't ever tell."

ಬಿಓಸ

Mevin's attraction was honest—not like the beer commercial kind on American television. He wasn't inflamed with desire, he just wanted to warm himself in this woman's presence. To be around her settled him. It was a better kind of desire. His eyes forced themselves to try and catch a glimpse or two whenever he thought she wasn't looking. His willpower limped to the back of his consciousness, and he was unable keep from trying to find her when she moved from sight. It felt good, this feeling he had. The numbness that still tingled on the edge of his soul ebbed. He discovered the sky bluer, the grass greener, and the East Tennessee biscuits and gravy almost edible. Nonetheless, he cursed the feeling. He fought against it. His life had almost drowned in despair. Now that he was in America, there was no need for it anymore. This woman was far beyond him. Her status and beauty left little hope. Besides, she was his best friend's sister-in-law. In this land, the importance of background was unclear to him. He did not know the effect that his feelings would have, and a friend of Ben's surety was worth more than an improbable love. So, Mevin decided to mute this feeling, to snuff it out, but on the way up the ladder, he looked at Lou again.

Later that afternoon, the rain came heavy and cut the day short. Claude's classes ran long on Tuesdays, so Ben asked Mevin to supper. The two piled in the pickup and drove from Kingsport to Mt. Carmel with the suspect aid of Ben's one good wiper blade. Pulling up into the Bellamys' long gravel driveway, they couldn't see well enough to make out the old Dodge Dart squatting next to the house. At the last moment, Mevin screamed a warning. Ben yanked the steering wheel hard right and crashed through the split rail fence, scattering cattle and tearing barbed-wire. The driver's side seat belt had long been broken, and Ben's head hammered the dashboard. Blood ran freely from a deep gash above his left eye.

"Doggone it! I made it all day without some kind of accident and now it comes right when I get home. I was hoping to tell Eloise to put that first-aid kit away for once."

"Are you all right?"

"Yes, it's nothing. I'll be all right in a minute." Ben dabbed at the gash with his forefinger then took a long look at Mevin. "You scream like a girl," he chuckled.

"I do not scream like a girl. I scream like an African warrior."

"Well then, African warriors scream like girls."

"Well, American roofers drive like dogs."

The two men laughed like they were the funniest people in the world. It might have been the adrenaline needing an outlet after the crash, or it might have been that they just lacked the same sense of humor. Whatever the reason, laughter still contorted them when they heard the rapping on the window.

༺༻

The Moonshine Brothers lived upon a small patch of dirt on the far side of Ben's property. Their clapboard house leaned heavily to one side, and it looked, from the road, like the dogs chained to the front porch had been installed just to hold it up. As the house aged, they added more dogs. It would have taken a man with a purpose to try and ring the front doorbell. Their women were long since gone, which seemed to suit the boys just fine. Each morning, they raised a confederate battle flag atop a stripped-down sycamore, then waded back through the dogs to a house of cold cereal, firearms and satellite TV. It was no place for a woman. A woman wouldn't stand for such coarseness. Like all folks, the Moonshine Brothers' lives were comprised of choices. And they had to choose to be who they were or who some woman might've wanted them to be. The boys chose the former. Consequently, female companionship was as common as a blue-moon Sunday.

The boys were really brothers, but although they came by it naturally, their last name wasn't really Moonshine. Nobody Ben knew could say for sure, or couldn't remember, what their genuine last name was. Moonshine was the call they came by, so Moonshine was what they were called. But it would have been easy to get the wrong idea. The boys weren't drunks. They were craftsmen. A reputation settled upon that old slanted house as being the foremost location for the acquisition of corn liquor. The boys never sold a drop. It was illegal to sell homemade brew, but they sure would trade with you. The boys were open to most anything: a satellite dish, a Browning, a beagle pup. The law tried to explain to them that trading amounted to the same thing as selling, but the

Moonshine Brothers never seemed to be able follow the finer points of jurisprudence.

Despite all that, Ben was proud to call them friends. And his friends were now rapping upon the window.

"You all right in there, Ben?"

"Yeah, Roy. I'm just fine." Roy was the younger of the Moonshines and a self-made expert in heating and air conditioning. Ben remembered Eloise saying that he was coming up to have a look at the heat pump.

"You don't look fine," the thin, creased face of Jack slid next to Roy and up against the window. Jack was the older of the Moonshines and a self-made expert in just about everything under the sun.

"I'm really fine. Step back a minute and let me get out."

Ben pushed the door open and stepped out onto the soft ground. "See, Roy, I'm good," he said, noticing the dryness gathering in the back of his throat. Taking a step to investigate the fence, his tingly foot trembled under his weight. "Doggone it," he said. And that was the last thing he said for a while.

༄༅

Scooping Ben's body off the soggy grass, the Moonshine Brothers had him up the stairs and into the house with animal-like swiftness. Eloise had them lay him on the bed, and they watched her tend to him for a minute or two before the urge to be helpful seemed to overcome their quiet curiosity.

"Is he going to be all right?" Jack asked.

"I think so. That's a nasty bump on his head. I'm going to get him comfortable and then go call the doctor's office. I think they'll still be open."

"Okay then," Roy said. "We're going to go get the truck loose and fix that fence before the cows get out."

"Thank you, boys. I'm glad you're here."

༄༅

Mevin lost the struggle with his seatbelt. The buckle jammed, and despite his best efforts, he could not free himself from it. He saw Ben fall and the men gather him up, and now he didn't know where any of them had gone. Desperation brought out the contortionist in him, and he managed to slither under the belt and out onto the floorboard. Yanking hard on the handle, he flung the door open and rolled out of the truck. Righting himself, he stood just as the men exited Ben's house.

ಬಿಂ

Ben came to and listened as Eloise talked to a nurse about his condition. There were a lot of "Yes ma'ams" and "I wills," but Eloise didn't do much talking otherwise. She cradled the phone and then came to his bedside.

"Look who is up."

"I almost made it through the whole day… the whole day… or at least a whole half a day."

"I know."

"What did the doctor's office say?"

"They told me just to keep an eye on you. Even though you never go to see them, they know how you are. They figure you'll be all right."

"If it wasn't raining so heavy, I believe I would've made it the whole day. Please let Mevin know I'm all right. He's prone to worry."

"Mevin?"

"Yeah. Mevin was in the truck. Didn't he come in?"

"No."

"Where are Jack and Roy?"

"They just went outside to pull your truck out of the fence."

"I've got to get up!"

In the better places of the world, "neighbor" meant more than proximity. East Tennessee was one of the better places.

The Moonshine Brothers loved Ben's family like their own, mostly because they were their neighbors. They visited often, and though they refused every invitation Eloise extended to come to church, they seemed to truly appreciate being asked. The boys wouldn't accept money for the work they did around the farm, so Ben and Eloise paid them in homegrown tomatoes and baked apple pies. Something seemed better about that form of payment anyway, and the boys seemed to appreciate that, too.

Ben knew The Moonshine Brothers would willingly die to protect the Bellamy family, just because they were neighbors, and maybe because they were also a little off in the head. And because of it, Ben held a deep fondness for the boys that he could only guess was similar to what siblings must feel. But Ben also knew that a man was made of different parts—some good and some bad. A decent man worked to grow his good and fence his bad. Only one man had ever lived without that kind of fence. So how you came to know a man was mostly dependent upon which side of the fence you found yourself. For all their good, the Moonshine Brothers had large patches of bad. Up to then, Ben had purposely kept Mevin away from the Moonshine Brothers' fence, and now he feared he was on the wrong side of it.

☙❧

The man in the green hat spoke in a low, even tone, but the rain muted the world with its intensity, and Mevin could not make out what the man had just said. "Excuse me. I did not understand you."

"Did you hear that, Roy? He says he didn't understand me."

"Step away from the truck," The other man, with no hat, said in a voice loud enough to settle any misunderstanding.

Maybe it was the rain, a kind of Burundian rain, but most likely it was the look. The men slinked toward Mevin with genocide in their eyes. Memory landed heavy upon Mevin's heart, and his body convulsed under its weight.

"What are you trying to do to our neighbor's truck?" The man in the green hat circled slightly to the left as he spoke. The man with no hat drifted to the right, bending down to gather a short piece of scrap wood as he went.

The men moved together as animals in a pack. Each seemed to sense the other's intention without speaking or even looking. They were used to fighting together, Mevin could tell, possibly even killing. Individually, they both looked dangerous, and together they were no doubt deadly.

"I was traveling with him." Mevin noted the movement of the man with no hat and angled himself to where he could see both men at once.

"Hear that, Roy. This old boy says he was in the truck with Ben. I didn't see nobody else in that truck. Did you Roy?"

"Nope."

"Mister. You are a liar."

Mevin strained to comprehend through the heavy rain and thick East Tennessee accents. "I do not understand you, completely. Please say again."

"Hear that, Roy. He still doesn't understand me. He's about to though. He's about to understand me real good. Isn't he, Roy?"

"I'd say so."

The voice of the man in the green hat startled Mevin. Green Hat was much closer than he had realized. Mevin thought about running, but decided he would run no more. In that moment, he set himself to fight. The sentiment was courageous, but deep down, as Mevin watched these men move, he knew that a sentiment was still all that it was. It wouldn't do a thing to save him.

※

"Sit down, Ben. You're wallowing around like a drunk man."

Ben lost his struggle against the dizziness. He collapsed along the wall then down to the hardwood floor. "I've got to get out there, Eloise. Mevin's going to be in some trouble."

"What are you talking about? It's just Jack and Roy out there. They're probably helping him out of the truck. They have no cause to hurt Mevin."

But Ben knew that causes were funny things. What caused one person to laugh made another cry. "You can't ever tell," he was fond of saying, but he believed he could tell now.

The Moonshine Brothers were likely to harm Mevin, and not because of any sort of racial bigotry. The Moonshine Brothers wouldn't hurt someone just because of skin color. It was more basic than that. What would cause the boys to move on Mevin was the fact that he was a stranger. Being black made him stranger still. Talking funny wouldn't help much either. The whole of Appalachia never had much luck with strangers, and every ounce of blood that coursed through Jack and Roy's East Tennessee veins told them to be wary. And Ben figured if they found Mevin hanging around their neighbor's truck, it would also tell them to be protective.

֍

"Let's see if we can help you understand a little better." Green Hat spoke loudly drawing Mevin's attention while No Hat moved in. Mevin felt the movement and readied himself.

"Hey. Hey. Hey! Mevin, Jack, Roy! Come see what I found." The shrill voice cut through the raindrops like a high-pitched cowbell.

Puckett stood atop a large pile of limestone. Mevin knew that the boy loved the rain and as long as it wasn't lightning and thundering, Eloise let him splash and stomp his way around the farm on rainy days. And now, there he was, eyeing the whole coming confrontation with a joyous smile pasted on his face. Overflowing from his hands was a large frog. And apparently, he was eager to show it off.

"Come on, boys. Take a look."

Encased in the oddity of Puckett's mutual recognition, Mevin and his adversaries stood frozen like plastic army men.

"Please hurry," Puckett pleaded. "He's squirming real bad."

Dutifully the men obeyed. Slogging up to Puckett's perch, they "oohed" and "ahhed" over the size of the creature.

"That's the biggest bullfrog I ever did see," Green Hat volunteered.

"Yeah, Puckett. You're a real frog wrangler," No Hat added.

"What do you say Mevin?" Puckett prodded. "Do they have frogs like this in Africa?"

"In all of Africa, I do not believe there is a frog with size such as this."

Puckett's grin was infectious, and the men found themselves smiling at each other. It was truly disconcerting.

Mission accomplished, Puckett leapt from the rocks and splashed through a large, mud puddle, toting his frog to parts unknown. Bewilderment fell with the rain. Puckett's excitement had stolen the energy to fight, and now, nobody seemed to know what to do. It was a bit late for formal introductions, and Mevin's adversaries didn't seem prone to apology. Mevin felt more uncomfortable than relieved.

They stood there for a full five minutes, trying not to look at each other. Like a bunch of shy little boys choosing silence over the risk of a misspoken word, they hadn't the wherewithal to make any sort of overture toward one another. It seemed that they all, even Mevin, craved certainty at the expense of understanding. They would have rather endured a sure fight than a vague peace. And as they stood there, that sad truth stood there with them. Not one of them had sense enough to come in out of it, or the rain.

Mevin believed that all of them, himself and thanks to Puckett, the two men he now knew as Jack and Roy, may just stand there forever. But then, the front door flung open and Ben stumbled out onto the porch. Eloise was close on his heels, but she couldn't catch him as he pitched forward. The men moved as one to help their friend and neighbor. Striding down from the rocks, they reached Ben and lifted him to his feet.

"Well. I see you boys have met," Ben said eyeing the men closely.

"Yeah, that's right." Jack said.

"Yes," Mevin agreed.

"Did ya'll exchange pleasantries?" Ben prodded.

"We hadn't quite made it that far, yet," Roy said, looking at the ground.

"Okay then. Sounds like I need to do some proper introductions. Mevin, these boys' names are Jack and Roy. But everybody sort of knows them as the Moonshine Brothers. And boys, this here is Mevin. Now that we got that out of the way, Eloise and I would love it if everyone would come on in and join us for supper."

"We can't, Ben." Roy apologized. "We've got something cooking back home. Don't want to leave it alone too long."

"That's right," Jack added. "We've got to get. But we'll be back later on to pull your truck out of the fence."

"Thanks boys. I appreciate you."

"We appreciate you, too, Ben," Jack said. "So long Eloise. So long Mevin."

Jack and Roy nodded their good-byes, and the two men left.

Mevin stood, stunned by the sound of his name upon the lips of his near enemy. Jack had spoken it as if, all of the sudden, it meant more than something to be conquered or destroyed. His eyes followed the figures down the gravel driveway. And then, he looked back from the Moonshine Brothers and toward his wobbly friend.

Ben smiled big at Mevin, then looked back down the driveway, "You can't ever tell," he whispered.

What You See and What You Get

Ben had really only ever been attracted to one woman—not counting the head turning type. Of course, head-turning attraction was also a part of the one that he had, but it wasn't the whole of it. It wasn't all there was to it. So if Ben was to count the kind of attraction that turned a head but also made a man feel honest and made him want to be a better man, it was only one. He'd only ever had one attraction like that. And even though he'd found it young, Ben knew that kind of an honest attraction didn't come along often. It was a gift. And if a man chose to reject it or if it somehow slipped away, he couldn't be certain it would ever be offered again.

A lot of men lived with the "what if" of an almost love. Although Joe never admitted it, Ben figured that's how it was for Joe and his Granny Catherine. It was painful. About the only thing a person could make of it was a good country music song. But even that was probably not worth it. So it was a wonder why a man, and for that matter a woman, would choose to ignore an honest attraction. Ben supposed it had a little to do with the fear of rejection. That was what folks tended to say anyway. But mostly, he guessed it came down to expectations. An expectation could be just as strong as fear. And, a lot of people either expected that object of their affection couldn't possibly share their feelings or that they shouldn't expect to have those sorts of feelings for a particular kind of person in the first place. So because of the expectations in their heads, they set out to deny what was in their hearts. But hearts aren't easily denied, and despite the wall of expectations standing between them, Ben sensed that Mevin and Lou were finding theirs particularly stubborn. And wedged between the heart and a hard place, he couldn't tell for sure whether the beginnings of their honest attraction would be cuddled or crushed.

Ben watched his two workmates watch one another and smiled. His head had cleared from the slight concussion of his car wreck—without the aid of a doctor. Eloise wanted him to go, but he put it off until the visit was no longer needed.

"At least take off work awhile. Just a couple of days," Eloise cautioned.

"I didn't even go to the doctor. And if I didn't even have to go to the doctor, it can't be bad enough to take time off work."

Eloise could find no way around such distorted logic. "Just be careful," she whispered.

"I'll be all right," he said.

Ben could not imagine not going to work. It just wasn't in him to lollygag. Besides, work was taking on a brand new entertainment value. After the pre-work prayer that Ben felt compelled to implement, he watched Lou watch Mevin before looking quickly away when Mevin turned to watch her. Ben would've had to be hogtied to keep him away from work. There was just a whole lot to watch.

Fall broke through the heat of summer, and the work dwindled to small jobs and patch-ups. Some years it turned that way, and some years it didn't. Ben and Lou were long past trying to forecast business conditions. And after watching the Twin Towers collapse on television, they were long past trying to forecast much of anything. When the jobs ran low, so did the crew. Ben and Lou kept the men working as long as they could, but every now and then they'd meet a stretch when the work just wasn't there. At those times, they'd keep who they could based on how long they'd been there. But that year was different. They'd worked non-stop through the summer, and in a fall filled with the emotional aftermath of the September 11 attacks, the two men on their long-standing crew were ready for some time off. The other, newer man had a daughter in Alabama whom he hadn't seen in four years, and he figured now was as good a time as any. There was no telling whether he'd ever come back. Ben met with them all before they left, but he spent a bit more time with the man headed to Alabama. After they talked, Ben prayed that this man would find what his father hadn't.

So that left only Mevin, and Ben rejoiced in silence. There was no way he could've kept Mevin on while letting the others go, but Ben had come to count on their wonderings as a natural part of what made a normal day special. The thought of them as being something out of the ordinary left him feeling empty. His friendship with Mevin wasn't a fragile thing, but he knew it still could grow brittle from neglect. Ben didn't want that to happen. Besides, from a purely business standpoint, Mevin was the best man he had. On a good day, he could even outwork Lou.

So there'd be just the three of them for a while. Ben wasn't sure whether that made Mevin's and Lou's inclination to watch more or less. Around noon, the brown bags were breached, the two men pulled up a piece of curb, and the wonderings began.

"I have a question for you, Ben."

"Shoot."

"How did you know that you were in love with your Eloise?"

Ben gave in to an easy smile. "Well, I suppose the first way I got the notion was the way I couldn't keep my eyes off of her. You know I just kept watching her all the time. I didn't want to seem like some sort of creep. But I don't know. I just couldn't stop looking over her way."

Ben's words struck Mevin's body with a paralysis, and the poor man couldn't seem to breathe. Finally shaking it loose, he began gasping for air, taking deep whistling breaths.

Ben couldn't hold it in. His shoulders shook from laughter while he tried desperately not to choke on his baloney and white-bread sandwich. Rolling to his side, he convulsed on the cold ground, knowing the whole time that if Lou saw him he was as good as dead. But that somehow that made it even funnier, and he struggled hard against himself to capture some sort of control.

"What is so funny?" Mevin demanded, "What is the reason for the laughter?"

Ben held his hand up in the universal sign of "give me a minute" then rolling back up to a sitting position, he put his arm around his friend. "You are the reason for the laughter. Well, you and that crazy sister-in-law of mine."

"Why is this?"

"Why is this? Because y'all are so obviously sweet on each other, but you're trying your darndest to stay sour."

"I am not certain what you mean by this sweet and sour."

"Do you like Lou?"

"Why of course."

"No. I mean do you 'like' like Lou. And don't give me any of that lost-in-translation nonsense."

Mevin gasped again, then as if only to keep Ben from laughing, in a whisper he answered, "Yes."

Ben let the answer lie. He was still smiling, but not from the silliness of it all anymore. He was smiling because when something so humbly sweet was said, there was no other reaction his body could make. "Well, she likes you, too. And I mean 'like' like."

"How can you know this?"

"I just know. There's a lot of goofy gawking going on around here, and you're not the only one doing it."

Mevin straighten and looked around for no apparent reason. "This cannot be so. Lou is beautiful. She is a woman of grace and purity. Her intelligence is beyond a scholar's. And I am just a refugee. An African refugee."

Ben shook his head and lost his smile. "Mevin, I need to tell you two things. I'll start with the first. I know you may find this hard to believe, because I do. But most men don't see what you see in Lou. I see it, but that doesn't count for much. I'm her brother-in-law, but really more like her brother. So my opinion doesn't count as a man's opinion. With Lou what you see and what you get are exactly the same. To me that's beautiful. But I suppose to a lot of men, it's just not. So it's not like Lou has suitors knocking at her door every night. That's the first thing. Here is the second. If I ever hear you refer to yourself as 'just a refugee' again, I'm going to knock your head off. In case you don't know that one, it means I will assault you physically. Do you know why?"

Mevin looked into the eyes of the friend now threatening him, "Tell me," he said softly.

"You are a man. And what I mean by that is you have gone through all this world can throw at a body and you're still here. You're still giving as good as you get. And you're not even aware of how much you've accomplished or how worthy of admiration you are. You're a tough humble, and there's nothing better than a tough humble." Ben looked into Mevin's eyes and saw something less than understanding. He drew a deep breath in search of an analogy.

"In America," Ben continued, "We like to play football. It's a beautiful game with all kinds of strategy and excitement. But the best thing about football is that it teaches you to get back up after you've been knocked down. It teaches you a tough humble. Am I making sense? Do you understand what I'm trying to say?"

"Almost."

"Almost? Goodness. I wish Joe Shelton was here. He's got a way with stringing words with meaning. Well, let me try again. There are people in this world who will wade through a river of trouble to get to what's right. And then there are people who will sit on the bank and worry over getting their socks wet. You, my friend, are soaked through and through. You have waded the river. You made it to the other side. And if that makes you 'just a refugee' then it is the highest compliment I know of. Do you understand me now?"

"Yes," Mevin said looking at his shoes.

"Good. So if you go disparaging yourself in that way again, I'll have to open up a can and straighten you out. Do you understand that?"

"Almost."

"Almost is close enough."

They sat together in silence, chewing their sandwiches and slurping Dr. Peppers.

"Ben?" Mevin broke the silence.

"Yeah, Mevin?"

"Will you talk to Lou for me about my feelings for her?"

The question caught Ben in mid-gulp, and Dr. Pepper spewed from his lips and out his nose. "Whoa there, Mevin. I don't know about that. Don't you think it would be better if you talked to her?"

"I am physically unable."

"Physically unable?"

"My mouth would not function if I tried to speak to her of my feelings."

"That is a problem. But I don't know. I mean, it may be better for you both if I just stayed out of it."

"In Burundi, we have an Umukuru w'umuryango. This is the head of the family. He appoints an intermediary to help in courtships. This is a necessary part of a good courtship, and I wish this to be a good courtship. Would you be my intermediary?"

"I wouldn't be a good one. I'm not really qualified. Besides, you're in America. An intermediary isn't required."

"For me it is."

"I don't know. To be honest, I'm a little afraid of talking to Lou about it."

"Do you think I am a good man?"

"Yes."

"Do you think I will be good to Lou?"

"Yes."

"Do you believe it is right that an African should find affection for a woman of light skin?"

"Mevin, I believe it's right for you to find affection for whoever strikes your fancy. I'm not going to lie. It might be tougher on you to find acceptance from folks than it would with an African woman. But as far as the rightness or wrongness—you are a Christian man, and she is a Christian woman. Faith is a better matchmaker than skin color ever will be. So, I believe it's as right as rain."

"Then it must be the fear of wet socks that keeps you from speaking to Lou."

Ben let go an easy smile. "You are a smart rascal aren't you? I'll tell you what, I'll talk to her and let her know that you are sweet on her a little bit. And then I'll come back and tell you what she says. But after that, I'm out of it. The whole thing makes me nervous for some reason. I'll be your intermediary, but only for a little while. Fair enough?"

"Yes. That is more than fair."

"Okay. But don't go getting impatient on me. I've got to get my head around this. I need to wait for the right time and formulate the right words. You know, find the right approach. It may take a little while."

"I have no other plans. I will be patient."

Ben slapped Mevin on the back, then grabbed his shoulder and shook it softly. "It might just work out," he said. Leaning into his friend, he stood, then quickly collapsed back to a sitting position. "My doggoned foot is asleep again. I can't seem to wake it up anymore."

"I hate to say it again, honey, but like I've been saying all along, it's bound to be a psychological problem."

Lou's voice startled the two men off the curb and into the street. They collapsed upon one another and lay in a heap.

Lou looked down at them, "You see what I mean. Look at you. Lying on top of Mevin in the middle of the street. You've got a psychological problem."

"You scared us. How long have you been standing there?"

"Scare easily, too? Best I can tell, you've got some kind sort of psychosomatic issue combined with an acute phobia for getting off your butt and back to work. And it looks like it's spreading to Mevin."

Ben untangled himself from Mevin and spread out supine atop the asphalt. "Is that right?"

"Yes, that's right. And I'd suggest that you go and see someone about your problem."

"Which one?"

"I'll take care of the phobia, honey. You needn't worry about that. But you need some extra help with that foot. You know what I'm talking about. Somebody needs to help you figure out why all of the sudden your foot bone is connected to your head bone."

"You think my foot is in my head," Ben said smiling from a prostrate pose.

"I do, honey. And if you don't get up, my foot's going to be connected to the opposite end."

A long period of silence fell upon them. Well, maybe it wasn't that long. But it was one of those times when good-natured banter teetered upon an angry line. Those kinds of times always seemed a little longer than they truly were. Ben looked up at Lou, and Lou looked down at Ben. Eyes locked and searched for an understanding of what the other was truly thinking. Then Lou looked quickly toward Mevin and back again. And though he knew it would light her red hair afire, Ben just couldn't hold it in. Laughter erupted from his sternum, unconcerned with his attempt to control it.

"What's so funny?" Lou almost yelled.

Again Ben held up the universal sign for "give me a minute" and was rewarded this time with a swift kick in the ribs. Air gushed from his lungs, but somehow he went right on laughing.

Turning on Mevin, Lou almost screamed. "He's hard to fire, but you're not. If you want to keep this job, I'd suggest you find somebody else to have lunch with."

For some reason that struck Ben as the funniest thing he had ever heard in his whole life. He howled. Eyes bleeding tears, he curled into a fetal position in the attempt to both cradle the laughter and protect his ribs.

Lou stared at him hard and said simply, "Psychological problem." Then turning sharply, she went back to the house, up the ladder and onto the roof.

It took a few minutes, but Ben was able to pull himself back to the curb and into a seated position. Mevin already sat, head hung low, downtrodden.

"Mevin, you look like somebody just shot your dog. What's the matter?"

Mevin looked at Ben in disbelief. "What is the matter, you ask? The matter is that it is of no use. Lou heard our conversation, and then she scolded me. She has no affection for me. And so you know, it did not help for you to laugh as a hyena in the night."

"No, I don't suppose it did. But I'll tell you what, my friend, Lou really likes you. And I mean 'like' like in a big way, much more than I thought."

"How can you see this? I do not see this."

"Well, I suppose even with Lou there is sometimes a difference between what you see and what you get. But I know her. She has great affection for you. And, I suppose I ought to go on and talk to her before she kills us both because of it."

Even though they were well-supplied with roofing nails, Ben gave Mevin the keys to his Ford and sent him after some more. Mevin still didn't have a driver's license, but he could drive. And, Ben figured the off-chance of Mevin getting caught by the police was far less dangerous than the certainty of his heart stopping out of nervousness over what was about to happen.

There was no reason to wait. Lou was mad, but she almost never stayed mad, at least not at Ben, for more than a minute or two. And if she was truly mad, no amount of time would make it any better. So screwing up his courage, Ben climbed the ladder and joined her on the roof.

"Howdy," Ben said.

"Hi," Lou responded flatly.

"Are you bent out of shape with me?"

"No, honey. Not anymore."

"Must have got it out with that kick to my ribs."

"Must have."

Ben let the noise of the neighborhood surround them. A dog yelped, wanting to come inside. Somebody finally got a leaf blower cranked up. And somewhere on a nearby road a diesel engine idled slowly. Ben always thought it funny what you could hear on a roof, up above it all. Most folks talked about what you could see from a high place, but Ben figured that hearing the music of everyday life lifting its way toward heaven to be just as important.

"Listen. I'd like to talk to you," Ben said in his naturally kind tone.

"Can't do it, honey."

"What do you mean you 'can't do it'? I thought you said you weren't mad at me."

"I'm not."

Ben scratched his head and shook his foot. "Then why won't you talk to me."

"Because of your foot, honey. All because of your foot."

"What about my foot."

"Until you go see a psychologist about your condition, I can't be sure that any talking you do won't be crazy talk."

Ben thought he saw a hint of a smile light in Lou's eyes. "That's crazy," he said.

"You would know," Lou countered.

"But I've got something very important to say to you, not like usual. It's something that you might even want to hear."

"I'm sorry."

Ben rubbed his face. "Well what if I just said it. You're standing right there, and you would hear it."

"I guess I would, but I wouldn't say anything back. You might as well be talking to the wind, honey."

"I sort of need you to talk back."

"That's fine, honey, because I sort of need you to go talk to the doctor."

"Do you really think I have some sort of psychological problem? I mean no kidding, do you really?"

"I'm not talking."

Ben shook out his foot again, trying to get some feeling. "I don't even know how to go about finding a psychologist."

"You've got an appointment over at Appalachian Mental Health in about 45 minutes."

"What?"

"I made you an appointment. In fact, I was just about to call and cancel it like I've been doing every day for the last couple of weeks."

Ben felt like he should be surprised, but he wasn't. Lou was smart. She waited on her way and eventually how to get it came along. "So you won't talk to me about what I need to talk to you about until I go get some mental health."

"You're getting better already, honey."

"Well, I guess we'll just have to take a vow of silence then, because I'm not going to do it." But almost before Ben got the words out, he heard the familiar rumble of his old Ford, and his will weakened. "Tell me the address."

"I thought you just said you weren't going to do it."

"I did. But like you said, I have a psychological problem."

ଽଠଽଓ

Ben found right off that there were two kinds of people keeping the seats warm in the waiting rooms of mental health professionals. First, there was the chin-to-the-chest-avoid-eye-contact-at-all-costs kind. Second, there was the over-jovial-glad-to-be-here-it's-so-good-to-see-you-my-name-is kind. Ben liked the first kind better. They may have been nuts, but at least they gathered enough sense to be embarrassed about their condition. They might have to come here, but they sure didn't want to stay. It probably pushed them to get on their horse and try and get better. The second kind probably never would. Maybe they didn't even want to. Ben decided being friendly in a psychologist's waiting room was a bad sign. And as a plump, balding man made the rounds searching for a partner in conversation, Ben prayed, *Oh Lord, please don't let that old boy talk to me.* Ben was too polite. He would respond to a stranger's overture, and then it'd be all over. Like a fish on a hook, he'd be reeled ever closer from a depth of silence and safety toward a surface too bright for comfort. But God was good, and he answered Ben's prayer. A long-legged brunette was more than happy to engage the plump balding man, and the two talked and laughed and generally made everybody else in the waiting room uncomfortable. Finally, Ben completed his paperwork and got called into the office. The thought of seeing a doctor had never made him so happy.

Lou had met Doctor Schilling at a Bible study. After the doctor's wife grew ill and died, he began to search—not for answers really, more for peace. And his search led him out from behind the rims of his psychologist's glasses and back to his boyhood faith. Lou said she really liked him, and that he was a kind man. They were friends and had been for a while.

"I wouldn't send you to a quack, honey." Lou had told Ben.

"Have you ever gone to see him? As a psychologist I mean?"

"I should've. There was many a time I think I should've. But no, I haven't. You shouldn't take a friendship professional anyway. Besides, I don't want anyone seeing me walk into a psychologist's office. They may think I'm nuts."

Ben was a little nervous when he crested the doctor's door, so he decided on honesty. Honesty was a fine antidote to unease. Keeping a guard up all the time was likely to drive a body crazy. Besides, Ben figured honesty might beget some answers. And for the $150 that Lou told him he was spending, he needed to give the opportunity for some answers a fair shot.

"Good afternoon," Doctor Schilling greeted him.

Doctor Schilling looked like his office—disheveled. Yellow legal pads lay about everywhere, papers stacked recklessly onto shelves threatened to fall, and a mound of notebooks fought for space atop what must have been a desk. The doctor wore a tweed jacket, but without those patches on the sleeves. His hair grew a rusty brown. He stood stooped and slightly on the short side. Wrinkles creased his face, and he seemed a little older than Ben thought he would be, except in the eyes. His gray eyes danced with a bemused intensity that reminded Ben of Puckett. His shirt escaped the left side of his corduroy pants and hung un-tucked over his belt. Ben liked him immediately.

"Good afternoon, Doctor," Ben responded in a clear voice.

"Please take a seat." Doctor Schilling motioned Ben to a large overstuffed chair.

"Thanks." Ben removed a jumbled stack of papers and eased down. Doctor Schilling plopped into a wooden straight-back chair and immediately tilted it backward. The two men sat across from each other sharing a slight smile.

"So tell me why you are here."

"Because of an African."

"Because of an African?"

"Yes, you can pretty much narrow it down to that."

"Well, widen it up for me a little then. Explanation takes a little meat on its bones. I don't understand such a skinny answer."

"I guess I could fatten it up and say that I'm here because I have a sleepy foot," Ben paused, "But it wouldn't be true."

"Then why could you say that?"

"Because my sister-in-law, Lou. You know her I think?"

"Yes. Very well."

"Okay. Well Lou thinks I have a psychological problem that keeps making my foot fall asleep. And she told me if I didn't come talk to you about my sleepy foot then she wouldn't talk to me about my friend, the African."

"She told you that."

"Well yes. But she doesn't know that it's the African she won't talk about. Not yet anyway. Are you following me?"

"Yes. I believe so."

"You're good."

"Well, thank you. But let me ask you this. Why doesn't your African friend just talk to her himself? And then you wouldn't have to bring your sleepy foot to me."

"Very good question."

"Well, thank you."

"My African friend is from Africa. And his custom is to use an intermediary to speak to a woman on his behalf."

"That would be nice to have."

"Yeah, it would. But the problem I'm having is that the woman I'm supposed to speak to, as my friend's intermediary, won't speak to me about anything until I speak to you about my sleepy foot."

"Let's speak of it then."

"Okay."

"When did it start falling asleep?"

"I don't know. A few months back. Maybe even longer. It could be even a year or so."

"When you say falling asleep, does that mean tingly and such?"

"Yeah sort of. But now that I think of it, it's not so much tingly as it is weak. Yeah, that's what it feels like, tired and weak."

Doctor Schilling gathered a yellow pad from the floor, dislodged a pencil from behind his ear and began writing. "Okay. You'll be pleased to hear that I don't believe you have a psychological problem. It most probably is a physical problem. I'm not a medical doctor, but I'd say you most likely have a problem with your circulation, but it also could be something more serious than that.

"I have written down the name and address of a medical doctor that I'd like you to see. Go see him first, and if I'm wrong and it's not a physical problem, then we'll examine your foot by way of your head. And since this first appointment has been so quick, if you go see this doctor and still need another session with me it will be on the house."

"Thanks Doctor Schilling, but I'll be all right. My foot will snap out of it. I appreciate your concern, but now that I've fulfilled my obligation to Lou, I can also fulfill the one to my African friend."

Doctor Schilling reached across the open space between the chairs and grabbed Ben's wrist. "Please go see this doctor," he said, forcing the piece of yellow legal pad paper into Ben's free hand. "Please."

ఠ⚭

Ben's visit prompted two phones to ring that night. The first came at the dialing of Doctor Schilling. It was a short, serious conversation, and it provoked the second call. Joe picked up his phone on the third ring and listened to the faraway sound of a familiar voice. "Of course," he replied. "I'll do my best."

Good Questions

Twelve months after the twin engine airplane carrying Mevin and Claude had landed at the Tri-Cities Regional Airport, the Outreach Committee welcomed its twentieth member. "That's it," Mr. Unsler announced. "We can't take anymore. Too many people, even good ones, make for bad decisions. We'll have to start a waiting list."

"Praise the Lord," Miss Emma proclaimed.

"Praise the Lord indeed," echoed Ben, putting his arm around the spry old woman. Then raising his arms he said, "All right folks, it's time to get started. Please take a seat if you can find one. Thanks.

"Let's start with a prayer. Dear Lord, guide and direct us. Show us what you want us to do. Help us to reach out and touch your will. Give us the strength to submit. Amen." The group responded with a resounding "amen" of its own.

"Okay, let's start with the Feeding sub-committee."

Mr. Unsler had helped Ben arrange the whole committee into sub-committees based on their function. "It will facilitate good communication, and the accountability will give us a bias toward action," Mr. Unsler had said with a certainty.

"I don't doubt it," Ben replied.

"The Feeding sub-committee has set up a Wednesday program in conjunction with The Salvation Army. We supply volunteers every Wednesday and Friday, as well as provide canned food from our weekly drives here at the church," Mary Hopkins, a tall, middle-aged woman with a heavy nasal tone took a deep breath and continued, "We have also partnered with Meals-on-Wheels, and we're staffing their program with volunteers from our church Monday through Thursday."

"What a great ministry, Mary. Is there anything the rest of the Outreach Committee can do to help?" Ben offered.

"Not that I can think of. God has blessed us in so many ways. Please just keep praying for us."

"We will, Mary, and thank you." Ben watched the tall woman sit and marveled. Mary Hopkins struck him as being an intellectual, hands-off type. She rarely spoke around the coffee and cookies after church, and most of the time she sort of stood in the corner appraising the crowd as if she were conducting a study. Now she was grabbing up volunteers like fish in a bucket.

Amazing, Ben thought, just amazing. And the amazement continued to blossom. Through the Building, Education, and Evangelism sub-committees, Ben sat in awe of the good work.

The meeting lasted over two hours, and Ben acknowledged to himself that the time had come to resign his chairmanship. He wasn't good at organizing large groups, or as Mr. Unsler said, "facilitating good communication." He took a kind of faith-filled pride in what grew out of his reluctant involvement with the original Outreach Committee, but now the committee deserved more than what he could offer. Even if he wanted to, he couldn't give it what it needed now. It just wasn't in him. So, another more gifted in the "getting things organized" department deserved the chance to live out their talent. Mr. Unsler was the obvious choice.

A change had settled upon Mr. Unsler so profound that it was physically visible. Still frenetic and a little too quick on the draw with his opinion, Mr. Unsler was nonetheless an altered man. In the twelve months since the landing of the plane, or maybe even a little before when he had stood up in church, kindness had struck a match in Mr. Unsler's eyes.

With each passing day, its flame rose higher. And this kindness seemed to give him a strength, or better still, an awareness of a truer way to go about things. The power of this awareness caused him to stand a little taller and appear a little trimmer around the waist. The whole effect was quite astonishing. All in all, it made him a more attractive man. And earlier in the month when Pastor Lumpkin had brought visitors from Chattanooga to observe his Outreach Committee, it was the power of Mr. Unsler's new attraction that had convinced them that they should leave.

"Excuse me, sirs," Mr. Unsler had said, attempting to corral the musings of a lanky, dour minister from a large suburban Chattanooga church, but was completely ignored.

Pastor Lumpkin had held court in a semi-circle of folding chairs with a half dozen other priests and pastors. They'd politely debated the combination of constraint and autonomy necessary for an outreach committee to properly function while the Outreach Committee itself began arriving for its weekly meeting.

"I have always believed," Pastor Lumpkin had said talking over the lanky, dour minister, "That you should not underestimate your congregation. Under the right guidance, outreach committees can do wonderful things. Witness what has happened with my Outreach Committee. They have the autonomy to follow their faith. Now, I'm not saying that they don't come to me for advice and guidance. Good heavens, do they ever." He'd given a roll of his eyes and forced a soft chuckle. The other ministers had chortled accordingly. "But, as a pastor, you have to have the faith that God will lead the sheep back to you when they go astray." The silence that follows a murmur of agreement had fallen upon the small assembly and given Mr. Unsler the opportunity to step into the middle of the semi-circle.

"Welcome to you all. We're glad that you came to see what God has led us to do. But if you want to stay, you're going to have to stand up. As you can see, people are filing in and we need your chairs. I'm sure you wouldn't want to disrupt our normal proceeding by sitting off over here by yourselves and taking our chairs."

Pastor Lumpkin had stared at Mr. Unsler with a look of pure disbelief. As if by instinct, he'd waved his hand in an attempt to shoo him away. But Mr. Unsler would not be shooed, not anymore. A discomfort had descended upon the group, one that didn't seem to bother Mr. Unsler in the least. And finally, the group of priests and pastors had stood as one and moved toward the back wall. Nodding and shaking hands with the assembled parishioners as they went, they had congregated briefly together before leaving during Ben's prayer.

Watching Mr. Unsler in action convinced Ben that he was the right choice to take over leadership of the Outreach Committee. The change in him made it so. And Miss Emma would be around to help keep him changed. Ben thought it wonderfully odd what could happen when a person, or a group of people for that matter, accomplished something that was illogical but nonetheless completely right. Afterward, folks tended to put logic in its proper place—a nice way to get around but not to decide where you were going. And, that's what happened to Mr. Unsler and the whole of First Communion. The Holy Spirit moved in, and the old way of making sense moved out. Ben figured the trick after that was to make sure the Holy Spirit stuck around, and that was always a tough trick. Folks tended to get way too smart for their own good. They'd figure and talk, and they'd talk and figure. The Holy Sprit didn't work too well if He couldn't get a word in edgewise. There was a need for folks to remain at least a little foolish—foolish in the faith. God was probably best heard by an honest idiot. And with Miss Emma's help, that's exactly what Mr. Unsler would be.

Ben reconfirmed in himself that stepping away from the Outreach Committee was the right thing to do. "Lord," he prayed, "Give me the sense to know when to call it a day. Help me not to get in the way of something I love." Limping back to his truck on a sleepy foot, he decided to talk to Mr. Unsler.

☼☾

"Now that's not right. I've kept my part of the bargain. It's only right that you keep yours."

"I'm sorry, honey, but I don't see it that way. You went. That much is true, but it's not much good if you don't follow the advice. If you don't follow the advice then what did you spend your money for?"

"I spent my money to keep my end of the bargain."

Ben and Lou stood atop a flat rooftop in Fair Acres. Soon they would set about rubber roofing again. But morning broke with a crispness that invited a little dawdling. Sometimes a day told them to slow down and watch it wake up. So they let a silence slide over them and waited for the day to stretch itself out of sluggishness.

Mevin had taken the day off. Or better said, Ben had taken the day off for him. East Tennessee State University was presenting Claude with an award for academic achievement, and it wasn't the type of thing family should miss just to install a rubber roof. At least Ben didn't believe it was, so he gave Mevin the day off with pay. Lou smiled at Ben's generosity and Mevin's thankfulness. Both men thought she had a beautiful smile, but neither dared to remove it by saying so.

"Oh all right, honey. I guess you're right," Lou said absentmindedly. "If you can't count on me to keep my end of a bargain, how can I expect you to pay me much mind about going to the doctor that Schilling recommended? I'm ready to talk with you, honey. But you best beware. I won't let up until you go see that other doctor. If your problem is not psychological it might be serious. You know that, don't you?"

"I'll be all right."

"I'm not going to let up."

"I hear you. And I know. But now, let's talk about something else."

"That was the deal."

Now that he didn't have to fight to be heard, Ben lost the capacity to speak. A nervousness seized his sternum and spread to his vocal chords. *I'm the world's worst intermediary*, he thought.

"Well…" Lou said, "I'm ready to do some talking."

Ben smiled at her helplessly.

"Ben? Are we talking or not, honey. Because if we aren't, we've got to get after it. This rubber roof isn't going to install itself."

Ben gave a soft croak, and then exhaled heavily through his nose.

"What is the matter with you, honey?"

"I'm nervous," he uttered softly. "I'm nervous," he said, again his voice gaining a little of its footing.

"Nervous. What in the world could you talk to me about that would make you nervous?" Lou's question tumbled from her mouth and laid on top of the roof for both of them to see. And they did, plain as day. They both saw the question just lying there.

"Well?"

"Well what?"

"Oh come on, Lou. You know what."

"I don't. I mean I can't."

"Can't what?"

"I can't get involved with a younger man."

Ben smiled and Lou gave in to one of her own, but it faded when she drew a breath to speak again. "Ben. I can't get involved with a black man."

"Who is talking about a black man? I'm talking about an African man."

"It doesn't matter."

"You're right. Because really, I'm not talking about that either. I'm talking about Mevin. Mevin… do you hear that, Lou? I'm talking about the kindest, strongest man I've ever met. I'm talking about someone who will care for you with all his heart and soul. I know this better than I know most anything. And I know you, Lou. You know it, too."

"I can't, honey. I just can't." Lou's voice cracked softly like a limb fighting against its own weight to stay attached to a tree.

The day crowded around them, and silence landed with a thud upon the roof. Ben knew it was no use trying to talk through a heavy silence, and he felt this being that kind of silence. The weight of some things was better left to another day or a different understanding. So, he turned to grab a large bucket of sealant.

"I'm not going to try and talk you into anything, Lou," Ben said over his shoulder. "Lord knows I'm not man enough to do it, anyway. But the thing I'd guess I would say, if I were to say something else, would be that we make our own can'ts. God only created the cans."

The day wore on in quiet. It wasn't an angry quiet with the occasional metered words and pointed politeness that often comes after an argument. It was more a hurting quiet, like the softness of sound that follows a funeral or the departure of a soldier for war. The waning sun brought them down from the roof and while Ben was packing gear back into his truck, Lou came and stood beside him. And when he placed his last tool in the corrugated box behind the cab, she extended her arms and hugged him. With strength that most men would envy, she pulled him hard to her chest and squeezed him long. Then, letting go without notice, she turned away quickly.

It seemed like something should be said; some explanation asked for or some comfort offered. But Ben knew better. Some things were better left unsaid, and other things just didn't need saying. It took most folks a lifetime of talking to figure that out.

ಸಂಪ

"You sold any of cows yet, Boy?" Joe said.

"Not lately. You written any songs, Old Man?" Ben responded.

"Not lately."

"Your cows are getting some age on them. What you are going to do when they start dying? Don't want to spend all your time digging cow holes."

"I'll cross that bridge when I come to it, I guess. How about you? Your songs are getting some age on them. What are you going to do when the royalties peter out? Can't spend all your time just figuring on the next good song."

"I guess I'll cross that bridge when I come to it, too."

The morning broke chilly, and a light frost gathered along the low spots, but the lack of color across the sky promised an oncoming clearness. The day would warm up nicely, and a promise of warmth was sometimes the only thing that would keep out the cold.

"Lou's gone." Ben said the words with the earnest matter-of-factness that somehow found harmony in the East Tennessee vernacular.

"Gone?"

"Gone."

"Where?"

"Oh. I'd say she's bound for the Florida Keys or maybe Panama City, whichever comes first."

It struck Joe that such a destination would make for a fine line in a contemporary country music song. But he kept the thought to himself. Ben looked to be good and low. It was not the time for an old man's musings about a song he'd never write.

"I talked to her just the other day," Joe said. "When did she go?"

"I'd guess she lit out last night. You talked to her?"

"You *guess*? Does that mean you don't really know whether she's gone?"

"I know. But I'll know for certain if she doesn't show up for work." Ben rubbed at his eye and exhaled, "She won't be at work, though. I guess I probably know that already. What did y'all talk about?"

"What chased her off?"

Ben let go another heavy breath. "It was something I said. Maybe I shouldn't have, but if it was going to make her go, she would have gone sooner or later."

"I see."

"Now tell me what y'all talked about before she left."

Joe let the question stand and shiver in the morning air. Ben found his eyes, but Joe couldn't look into Ben's for long. Kicking at the dirt, Joe reached down and picked up a rounded rock and sort of tossed it from one hand to the other.

"If you don't have a mind to, you don't have to tell me, Joe" Ben said, still searching for Joe's eyes.

"It's not the mind that I'm lacking, boy. It's the heart."

ಬಂಚ

Lou didn't turn up for work. And after they said the pre-work prayer, Ben and Mevin sort of milled around a while, just waiting. They tried on a look of anticipation, but they didn't wear it well. They'd never beat Lou to a job site before, and they knew they hadn't now. Sooner or later, honest folks grew tired of pretending. Ben and Mevin were honest folks.

"It is my fault," Mevin's voice fell out of his mouth in monotone.

"It's not your fault. It's mine. I'm a lousy intermediary."

"No. It is my fault. I have shamed her with the acknowledgment of my affection. She can no longer bring herself to look at me."

Ben took a long look at his friend then put a strong arm around him. "Sometimes we do nothing, because we're afraid something might happen. Lou's never been good at doing nothing. She had to do something, so she left. It's more because of herself than because of you."

Mevin returned the long look and filled it with a load full of silent questions. Ben shrugged and the two men turned toward their work.

That day they weren't worth shooting. Sometimes a loss will cause a person to throw themselves into their work. This wasn't one of those times. They slogged around like turtles in creek mud. Every so often, Ben would shake his foot, but that was the extent to which either expended any vigorous energy at all. Neither spoke much, and the morning stood still just to watch their quiet.

"Let's call it a day," Ben said mustering the courage to surrender.

"It is only 10:30."

"I know, but we aren't getting a thing done. Besides, I'm supposed to meet Joe Shelton back at his house around lunch time. I'd planned on just half a day anyway."

"Okay," Mevin said, putting up little resistance.

In slow motion, they cleaned and cleared the site and piled into the Ford. "I know Claude's off at school, so why don't you come over for a while?" Ben tried to sound upbeat then quit the attempt in mid-sentence. "You can talk to Eloise and Puckett while I go see Joe, and then we'll eat lunch and go fishing. I've been meaning to take you, and with this little bit of a warm spell it should be a good day for it."

"I think I will go home."

"It's not a good day to go home by yourself. Come on and go fishing. It'll cheer us both up."

"Thank you."

ಸಂಲ

At the gate earlier that morning, Joe told Ben to come back to his house later so that they could talk. Joe tried to believe that the reason he did was so that Ben would know how important the conversation was supposed to be. It wasn't just a gate conversation. It was something more critical, something that required a special visit. Joe tried to believe that he was attempting to elevate the seriousness of the conversation so that he would be better able to get through to Ben. When Joe was younger, he could talk himself into believing what he wanted to. But now that he had a little age in his eyes, Joe couldn't blind them as easily, and all he really saw in himself at the gate early that morning was fear. And as Ben knocked on his door, Joe leaned heavy on a faith that he prayed would be better than that fear—at least for a little while.

ಸಂಲ

Mevin stood in an empty house. Eloise and Puckett were nowhere to be found, but that was not unusual. Ben said that Eloise had no way of knowing that he would knock off early from work, so she and Puckett went about their day, probably to the grocery store or maybe the library. Puckett liked the library. Ben promised to be back soon, and then he had left for Joe's.

Uncomfortable in another man's house alone, Mevin went outside and sat on the porch to keep company with his aching heart. Just sitting made him feel pathetic, so he pulled himself up and strode down the long field toward the copper-colored river that cut its way through the limestone and slate. The river flowed shallow in the winter, and Mevin wondered what kind of fish would be hardy enough to survive in such a small patch of water amongst so many rocks.

Looking deep into a small pool in search of any sign of life, Mevin's intensity was interrupted by the sound of splashing. Turning toward the disturbance, he squinted upstream, trying to place the noise. Mevin saw the white flash immediately and was amazed by the size of the fish. But as he watched longer, he determined it was not a fish at all, but rather some type of animal. Interested if for no other reason than it distracted his heartsick boredom, he watched closely as a furry white animal floated toward him.

The creature made its way around rocks and through rapid water flows by swimming in a tumbling fashion near the middle of the river.

"What an odd method of transporting oneself," Mevin said aloud.

The animal drew nearer until it floated, not ten feet away, right past Mevin. And as it crossed his path, the animal struggled to break the water before releasing a small yelp and tumbling back under. Mevin stared after it for a moment before the recognition finally broke past the absurdity.

"Dog!" Mevin yelled. "It is a dog."

It was actually a puppy, but such a small distinction in times of consequence was of no importance. And Mevin felt that this was just such a time, at least for the puppy. Leaping from the bank, he splashed his way down the river in a modest version of hot pursuit. The river's current pinned the pup against a large boulder and literally began to wash the life out of it. Mevin took advantage of the pause in progress and gained upon the limp animal. Grabbing the dog by the loose skin behind its neck, he held it aloft and made for the bank. By the time he reached the shallows, the pup squirmed back to life, whining vigorously over its rough treatment.

"Oh come now, it will be okay," Mevin said stepping from the water. "You are fine now, little one. All is okay."

"What are you doing with our dog?" the voices sounded a flat harmony that caused Mevin to teeter backwards. It was a harmony he'd heard before—one that lived only between the Moonshine Brothers.

☙ღ

"Come on in, Ben. Sit down. I've got some coffee made. I'll be right back," Joe said with what he hoped was a level voice.

Ben took a seat in the same rocker he had ridden as a little boy. Easing into to it, he let go a soft smile. "I used to love this chair," he called after Joe. "I remember Granny Catherine fussing all the time that I was going to break it if I didn't stop rocking so hard. It never did break, though. I guess some things are just made hard to break."

"You can have it," Joe said returning with two large mugs of steaming black coffee.

"What?"

It was too much. Joe knew it as soon as he said it. His emotions were already way out in front of his good sense. There was nothing else to do but forge ahead. "I said you can have that rocker. It's not doing me any good, and I know you like it. I should have given it to you a long time ago."

Ben blew on his coffee and eyed Joe over his mug. Then he took a long slurpy sip and said, "It's all right, Joe. Everything will be all right. Just tell me what's on your mind. I'm guessing it's not some new song you finally got around to writing."

Joe looked at Ben and thought how it was a wonder that honesty seemed to be the last hand dealt, even by decent people. Sooner or later though, everybody deals their own last hand. And it's the decent people who find it in themselves to go on and play it out. Joe always thought of himself as decent people. "No, it's not a song, Ben," he finally managed to say. Then drawing a ragged breath, he continued, "It's that I think you might be sick. I think you might be bad sick."

"What makes you say that, Joe?" Ben broke into a wide, warm smile. "I'm as healthy as a horse. Matter of fact, I'm as good as I've ever been. I haven't fallen down or bumped my head in weeks. I'm about ready to tell Eloise to put all those first-aid kits away. There's nothing wrong with me except…"

"Except that foot of yours that always seems to be asleep," Joe interrupted, finishing Ben's thought in the sort of abrupt way that comes from either anger or concern.

"Yeah, that's right, Joe," Ben's warmth never left him. "Except for this silly foot. But it'll be all right after a while. It will be all right."

"I don't know, Ben. It might be something serious."

"Oh Joe, it's nothing…"

"Listen to me, boy," Joe interrupted again, this time with more force than before. Tears came from somewhere beyond his control, and he had to force his voice to even out. "Lou set you up to go to Doctor Schilling so he could hear about your symptoms, not so he could hear about your problems. Doctor Schilling's wife died of a serious illness, and her illness started out with a sleepy foot. Doctor Schilling doesn't know if you have the same illness or not, but he does know that you ought to get checked out."

Ben blew into his coffee again. "Lou sent me to the psychologist so that he could decide whether or not I needed to go see a regular doctor?" he asked smiling broadly.

"Yeah, she did."

"Why didn't she just send me to a regular doctor in the first place?"

"You've never been to one before—at least not for a long time. So I guess Lou figured it'd be easier to get you to go to a doctor about your head than it would be to go about your body. Besides, even if you did go, you might go to the wrong doctor. Lou tells me that most doctors don't know much about this kind of illness. You might choose the wrong one. And then, who knows what the diagnosis would be. Lou figured you didn't know any psychologists. She figured she could steer you toward Doctor Schilling. And then, he could steer you toward the right medical doctor."

"Well, I'll be. Lou is a sneaky rascal isn't she, a smart sneaky rascal. Why did she get you to tell me about it?"

Joe left that question alone for a minute while they both sipped at their coffee. And then, though the tears paid no heed, he smiled. "Well, she told me you would listen to me better than to her. And she said that it'd be best for someone other than Eloise to try and convince you first. She didn't want Eloise worrying over what's probably a whole lot of nothing. But I've got a notion, it's because she knew I would cry. I'm thinking she was betting on the fact that you wouldn't be able to stand up to an old man's tears."

"Lou is a good one," Ben said. "She's only been gone a day, and I've done a year's worth of missing her already."

Now that his coffee no longer crowded the top the mug, Ben rocked long and easy in the chair. He kept his quiet while Joe rubbed his nose on his shirtsleeve, trying to gather some sort of control over himself. "Well," Joe said finally.

"Well what?"

"Are you going to do it?"

"No. I don't believe I will. I'd rather this chair stay right here. But I'm going to make a point of getting Puckett over here more often so he can do his best to wear it out."

"That's not what I'm asking."

"It's not?"

"Come on, Ben. Are you going to go see this doctor or not?"

"Yes sir, I'll go see him." Ben didn't pause the rocker or show the slightest hint of aggravation. He would go, Joe knew, not for himself, but for Joe and for Lou.

"What is it that Lou and Doctor Schilling suspect I have?" he asked softly, still rocking.

"It's acting a lot like Lou Gehrig's disease. Lou learned all about it while Doctor Schilling's wife was struggling with it. Do you know anything about it?"

"I've seen the movie."

"Well, it's probably not that, anyway. It's just best to check it out."

"Yes sir, I agree. But I'd appreciate it if we kept this between us. Lou was right not to tell Eloise, yet. I don't want her and Puckett to worry. And if Eloise knew I was going to the doctor without the help of wild horses, she'd worry. I'll tell Mevin, though. I'd sort of like him to know"

"I won't say a thing."

"Thanks Joe. Thanks for everything, especially the tears."

"Don't go telling on me about that."

"I wouldn't think of it. Hey, how about coming down for lunch?"

"I've already been invited."

Ordinary Things

Jack stepped from behind a scraggly sycamore, and Roy appeared between the tumbling rocks of the river bank. "What are you doing with our dog?" the Moonshine Brothers asked again in an unnatural unison. The tones of their voices regained the menace of their initial meeting. Gone was the inflection of friendship that was present when Ben was around. And this time, it was certain that Ben would not be around.

Mevin set the puppy gently to the ground, and Jack's sharp whistle drew the animal to him. Mevin watched the pup's obedience and decided against it for himself. Like before, he was ready to fight—just plain old tired of trying to be nice. Even a good man was bound to get that way in the midst of being wet, cold, and heartbroken. But even through his heartbroken resolve, Mevin still understood that being ready to fight didn't make a man a good fighter. Fighting made a man a good fighter, either that or having more to fight for than the other man. And it was debatable whether being tired of being nice was more of a reason to fight than being just plain mean. What wasn't debatable was the fact that the Moonshine Brothers were fighters and Mevin was not. In storybooks, such realities didn't matter, or at least they were ignored. But Mevin figured that the people who wrote storybooks hadn't been in many fights. So as he stepped forward, he succumbed again to the notion that he was about to be beat-up. But, Mevin also understood something else that eluded writers of storybooks. Mevin understood that there were worse things.

"Listen closely to me, moonshine men," he said with an honest attempt at making his molasses accent sound menacing, "I have just now saved your dog. If this is a reason to fight me, so be it. I am ready to fight. I have no reason to be afraid. The woman of my affection has left town. I am tired. I am wet. I am heartbroken. When we fight, be assured I will give you a good one. I have lived in a country of fighting. I have seen what fighting means. But let's not stand here looking at one another. If we are to fight, let us be on with it. Let us be on with it now." Mevin raised his fists in the manner he'd observed in late-night movies.

His eyes never leaving Mevin, Jack bent down and picked up the shivering puppy, but Roy strode along the riverbank with a purpose. Mevin calculated that he would have to fight Roy first, and with fists still raised, he turned toward the approaching moonshine brother.

Roy moved upon Mevin quickly and in a single swift motion swatted his fists away like a pair of troublesome flies. Still moving forward, he grabbed Mevin roughly and squeezed him hard between strong wiry arms. Mevin waited for the pain, perhaps a cracked rib or a knife to the kidney, but no such harm befell him. It took a while standing like that, his arms pinned against his body by Roy's iron grip, before Mevin realized that Roy wasn't trying to harm him at all. In fact, Roy was actually hugging him. The awareness struck him with more fear than the thought of the fight.

Mevin and Roy stood hugging by the river for what seemed like an eternity, and the whole time Mevin kept hoping that Roy's affection would progress no further. Finally, Roy broke loose and stepped back.

"Thank you, mister. Thank you for saving our dog," he said.

"It's my favorite one," Jack chimed in.

"Now," Roy continued, "If you feel like we need to fight, let's fight. I don't much want to with you saving our dog and all, but if you feel the need to I'd be happy to oblige. It's the least I can do." With that, Roy reared back and landed a crushing left cross to Mevin's chin, knocking him down the bank and back into the river with an impressive splash.

"Wait!" Mevin yelled rising from the water and trying to find his balance between moss-covered rocks. "I do not wish to fight! I do not wish to fight!"

"Good," Roy said, offering Mevin a hand and yanking him from the river. "Good," he said again slapping him hard on the back.

"Good," Jack echoed from beside the scraggly sycamore.

"Good," Mevin agreed, the weight of the world lifting from his shoulders.

They stood there smiling at each other and not knowing what else to say. "I'm sorry about your woman running out on you," Jack said, finally breaking the silence with a clearness of sincerity that shook Mevin from whatever perception he had formed about the man.

"You can't never tell about women, that's for sure." Roy put his arm around Mevin's shoulder. "Dogs are more knowable. It's easier to talk to a dog."

"Yes," Mevin agreed, "Dogs make for fine companions."

The brothers smiled at the harmony of sentiment, and Roy said, "Come on up to the house, Mevin, and we'll get your clothes dry."

It was not lost on Mevin that Roy called him by name again. And the natural warmth of the invitation echoed a peace that Mevin believed the Moonshine Brothers did not offer falsely. "Yes, thank you. I have an invitation to lunch, and I would like to be dry first."

"Good. So as you might remember, my name's Roy and this here is Jack. As you know folks call us the Moonshine Brothers, so that might be how you know us better."

"Oh," Mevin said alarmed, "When we were readying to fight, I'm afraid I mistakenly referred to you as Moonshine Men."

"Moonshine Men," Jack repeated, "Sounds like we're superheroes."

"Don't matter," Roy said, meeting Mevin's eyes with a goodness he hadn't seen before. "From now on, Jack and Roy will do fine."

༄༅

Joe and Ben rolled up the driveway in Ben's F150. Deacon Grainger's Dodge stood neatly in Ben's place. Joe smiled to himself and snuck a sideways look at Ben.

"Oh brother," Ben exhaled.

"What's the matter, boy? Didn't you know that Eloise was having a couple old men over for lunch?" Joe laughed out loud, and it felt good.

"No, I didn't. She doesn't know that I'll be home. I hope it doesn't mess up her plans."

They took the steps together, then Ben allowed Joe to go through the front door first.

"Well," Eloise said with genuine excitement, "I didn't know you would be home."

"Well, this old man," Ben nudged Joe with his shoulder, "found me and said this was a good place to scare up a meal. But if he'd told me how good looking the women were, I'd been here sooner."

"Dad!" Puckett hollered, leaving a checkers game with the deacon and rushing to his father. Ben lifted him to his shoulder and spun him around once for good measure.

The deacon stayed at the checker board, waiting for Puckett's return. "Good to see you, Mr. Grainger," Ben called.

"Yes. Yes. Good to be here," the deacon responded.

Ben and Eloise wandered toward the kitchen and with the fresh glass of sweet tea Eloise handed Joe, he went to check out the checkers game.

"Never, never leave a game in progress." Joe came upon the deacon leveling a stern but quiet scolding on a moist-eyed Puckett. "Do you understand me?"

"Yes sir," the little boy nodded.

It was almost more than Joe could take, but he had given up confrontation about the same time he had given up song writing. So, Joe just settled in the chair next to Puckett and asked, "How are you fairing, boy?"

"Not so well," Puckett said perking up a little.

"The deacon's got you on the run, I see."

"Yes sir, he sure does."

"Do you mind a little help?"

Puckett looked quickly to the deacon, but Joe wasn't having any more of it. "Oh, I'm sure the deacon won't mind. Seeing that you're only near about five or six and he's near about… well, he's just plain near about ancient."

The deacon released a grim smile at the comment, but Joe continued. "You don't mind me helping the boy out a little, do you Deacon? Just a couple of moves is all he really needs help with anyhow."

"That's all he needs, huh."

"As far as I can tell, yes."

"Well, help him then."

Joe loved checkers. To Joe, checkers was like a well written song—simple but with layers of meaning that revealed themselves the more it was played. And Joe had played a lot. If there was such a thing as a professional checkers player, Joe believed he might have made the majors. It sounded silly, Joe knew, a professional checkers player, but he figured it was no more outlandish than a professional songwriter. So as Joe eyed the board with its handsome red and black squares of complex simplicity, he figured the deacon was three honest moves away from a sizable helping of humility.

☙☛

With Jack and Roy's help, Mevin navigated through the pack of chained dogs that held fast to the slanted house. Every second or third animal they passed, Jack would point to and say, "That's my favorite one."

"He ain't right when it comes to dogs," Roy explained.

The front door hung open, and the trio entered. "Take off your clothes and we'll hang them on the heater," Jack said, while picking up newspapers off the floor.

Mevin looked to Roy, who nodded his agreement. So, Mevin stripped down one piece of clothing at a time and handed them to Jack who spread them on the newspapers and then laid them across a large collection of pipes that provided the boys with steam heat.

"Good Lord, son, not your under-drawers," Jack stepped back. "You're gonna scare me, Roy, and the dogs. Let's let those dry right where they are."

Mevin was embarrassed by his mistake, but only slightly. Mostly he was cold. Wringing wet and now standing in the middle of the draft-ridden slanted house in nothing but his red boxer shorts, his body gave way to the shivers.

"Oh, I'm sorry," Roy said, noticing Mevin's predicament. "You must be freezing cold. Let me go get you something." Roy left the room, leaving Jack and Mevin smiling at one another, but he returned in short order holding a mason jar filled to the top with a clear liquid.

"This will warm you right up," Roy said, handing the jar over to Mevin.

"It'll help with your hurting heart, too," Jack added. "At least for a little while."

Mevin held the jar close to his bare chest and thought about giving it a sniff but didn't want to offend his new friends by inspecting their offering. He figured it to be some sort of water-based concoction, probably loaded with sugar to give his body energy and, therefore, heat. All in all, he would have preferred a heavy coat or even a cotton shirt, but when Roy said, "Go on, drink up," Mevin obliged.

Heat exploded down Mevin's esophagus and oozed its way through his chest and down into his stomach. At first it was like a stovetop burn, something that a nervous system recoils from. But by the time it reached his toes, it was more like the warmth of a thick blanket, and Mevin's whole body began to snuggle right into it. Mevin had tasted alcohol before, mostly wine as a child and from one or two clandestine pulls on a bottle with a fellow student in Burkina Faso, but East Tennessee moonshine was different.

Corn liquor, sometimes referred to as "Mountain Dew", had been reported to run automobiles and light small cities for days. Some said it came straight from the rivers of hell. Others claimed it was no more than a poor man's magic elixir. With that particular liquid, what eased the pain of one man was likely to kill another. With any hard liquor, especially corn liquor, it was tough to figure what a particular person's reaction would be. Regardless of their disposition while sober, some folks seemed to get happy, others got sad, and some got just plain mean, but most, if not all, had a hard time just holding the stuff down the first time they imbibed in more than a sip or two. So it was nearly a miracle that Mevin didn't choke, cough, or spew the liquid fire entering his body across the walls of the slanted house. Even to the well-initiated, it took a little preparation before ingesting corn liquor. Some folks sort of spun around, some sounded heavy sighs, and a few whooped like an injured animal. But most everybody sort of needed to work themselves up a little before melting their insides out. Of course, Mevin was drinking the Moonshine Brothers' brew, and most likely the smoothest, easiest tasting liquor ever made without some sort of label on it. Nonetheless, it took a lot of natural talent to take two full chugs from a mason jar of clear hot lava without so much as a gritted tooth.

Mevin lowered the mason jar and eyed Jack and Roy. "You are good men," he said in a voice that he seemed to have borrowed. Then, quick as a whip, he tipped the mason jar up again.

"Whoa, son." Roy stepped forward and plucked the jar from Mevin about halfway into a fourth gulp. "Be careful with that."

"I am trying to be warm."

"I believe that's warm enough." Roy held the jar up, showing Jack the contents. It was less than a quarter full.

"Wow!" Jack whistled.

Mevin stood stock-still, watching Jack and Roy from a place his mind had never traveled before. An elation took hold of him and filled him with a sense of purpose. But unfortunately, Mevin kept forgetting what that purpose was. So he kept standing there, in a place that seemed to be outside of his own body, trying to corral that purpose. The brothers went on about their business, moving around the house and talking idly. They'd no doubt witnessed just about every effect corn liquor invited. A tall frozen African man standing in their living room didn't seem to faze them in the least.

"You are good men," Mevin yelled with the full force of his lungs interrupting a conversation Jack and Roy were having about a new beagle pup.

"Thank you kindly, Mevin," Roy said, shooting a look toward Jack.

"Hey Mevin," Jack chimed in, "Why don't you lie down a while?"

"Very good," Mevin answered, and sprawled himself face down on the floor, but only for a minute. Drawing his arms in, he pushed himself up quickly. "You are good men," he proclaimed once again to Jack and Roy. "Have you met my brother, Claude?"

"No. I can't say as we have," Roy responded.

"He is a good man, too."

"I'm sure he is."

"And Ben Bellamy… have you met Ben Bellamy? He is a very good man. Much like my father. I must see him now and tell him that he is a good father. Au revoir, Moonshine Men." And without further ceremony, Mevin hurled his nearly naked body out through the front door and in amongst the pack of semi-wild dogs attached to the slanted house.

Jack and Roy sat silent at the exit. Staring together at the space between them, it was Jack who spoke first. "I believe he's going to try to make it through those dogs."

"I believe you're right," Roy nodded his agreement.

"If he makes it, where do you suppose he'll go?"

"Sounds like he's planning on seeing, Ben."

"In his under-drawers."

"Drunk as a cat."

"That should be a sight."

"If he makes it through those dogs."

Mevin agreed with the Moonshine Brothers' appraisal that dogs were one of God's best animals. Almost unflappable in their loyalty to a loving hand and a regular bowl of food, those that loved and fed their dogs had no fear of physical harm, at least not if the dog could help it. But a stranger had best beware of sudden moves. It took a bold man to approach a dog-laden house without the presence of its master. A dog was always at the ready, constantly about its loyalty. But it was still possible for a dog to be surprised. It was feasible, and actually all together likely, when a drunken African man, wearing only red underwear, came running from an old slanted house in the middle of Appalachia, it could catch a dog off-guard. It was just not something that a dog could be expected to anticipate. And that bunch of dogs didn't.

Mevin ran through the canine minefield before the first hound looked up. And when he did, it seemed that it took that particular dog a while to understand what had just happened. In fact, he looked to the dog beside him and almost shrugged. But the dog on the other side caught a whiff of something and went to braying and tugging against his chain, bound and determined to set off after whatever it was that just ran by. That set the whole bunch off, and in a matter of seconds, all manner of dogs were letting loose with their Sunday-best howls. Jack and Roy rushed out to investigate, but by that time, Mevin was long gone and heading up Ben's driveway with the single-though-cloudy-minded purpose of telling him that he was a good father.

&CB

Joe moved the red checker and watched the deacon move his black one in the manner that he had expected. Playing checkers didn't invite much psychological nuance. Personalities tended to play out on the board just like they did in life, and it didn't even matter which color you played with. You could learn a lot about a person by the way they played checkers. One trick to winning was knowing your opponent before the game started. Knowing yourself helped, too. The deacon followed suit with the second move, and it wasn't until Joe reached for the third that the deacon realized how much trouble he was in.

"Hold on there," the deacon protested. "This game is between me and Puckett. Let the boy finish the game."

"All right Deacon, you're right," and then turning toward Puckett Joe said, "He's all yours, Puckett."

Puckett reached toward the board then drew his hand back. Joe prayed with all that he could muster that Puckett would make the right move and lock his sorry grandfather into a no-win and humiliating series of jumps and double-jumps. Joe understood without being told that to pray for such things was not proper and certainly something less than Christian. Joe offered no excuses besides the sure knowledge that God wanted Puckett to beat his sorry grandfather, too.

Puckett was going to do it. Joe saw the recognition ripple through his little body. The deacon saw it, too, and his face flushed red. *Thank you, Lord,* Joe thought loudly. Puckett's hand hovered over the right red checker, and he was just about to slide it on to glory when the front door burst open.

Mevin stumbled to his left. Then, seeing the crowd around the checker board, he made a hard right. Everyone looked up at the remarkable sight—Mevin standing over them like some noble drunken warrior in red underwear. And like the Moonshine Brothers' dogs, it took them all a while to comprehend what was happening. Joe was just noticing the symmetry between the red and black of Mevin's appearance and the red and black of the checker board and thinking how it wouldn't be all that tough to make such a complicated connection in a folk music song, when Mevin raised his hand to indicate that he was about to speak. And Joe thought he was. Joe thought they all thought he was. But he just stood there, with his hand raised, words seeming to crowd against the back of his lips. And they just sat there looking up at him, waiting for those words to be let out. Then, in a mighty red and black crash of naked flesh and rounded plastic, Mevin collapsed right down upon the checkers game.

The deacon did not seem happy. He stood in the corner, shaking his head slow and deliberate. The ruckus brought Ben and Eloise running, and Ben dragged Mevin by his feet out the door and toward Puckett's bedroom. Such disarray did not sit well with the deacon. Proper places were disrupted. Proper conduct had been abused. Some found that funny, others only unforgivable.

Joe tried to put a good face on it. Sidling up to the deacon, he whispered, "You reckon that was how it was answered?"

"What?" the deacon whispered back.

"Your prayer."

"My prayer?"

"Your prayer that Puckett wouldn't make the right move with his checker."

Joe meant it to be funny—well mostly funny—but the deacon couldn't find the humor. "I assure you, sir," he said leveling his voice right at Joe, "that I do not pray for things as meaningless or as an ordinary as a checkers game."

Joe stood there a minute, thinking that he should tell the deacon that, the best he could tell, prayer brought meaning to ordinary things. And ordinary things brought meaning to life. And maybe, if he'd be a little less formal with the Lord and more giving of himself, he could find the grace in ordinary things like letting his grandson beat him at checkers. But, like Joe had thought earlier, confrontation had left his barn a while back. Besides, he was in another man's home speaking to one of his guests. He had no right to call the deacon out. And honestly, he wasn't sure he was in the right, anyway. So he just nodded and moved on into the other room.

There was a hushed and hurried conversation between Eloise and the deacon, and soon after, he left. Joe thought Eloise might be upset, but she seemed more relieved than anything.

"Let's eat," she called, and Ben, Puckett and Joe sat down to break bread.

They talked, laughed and ate. Good things came in threes, and Joe believed there was hardly a better trio. The beauty of it all struck him hard, and he began to tear up a little.

"Oh Lord," Ben cautioned, "don't start doing that."

But Joe couldn't help it and a teardrop slid down his cheek and splashed upon Eloise's good china. Puckett was seated beside him, and he gave Joe a good looking-over before he stretched his little arm around Joe's back. That was too much for everybody. Eloise started crying, and though Ben was not given to tears, the weight of the day must have set upon him, and he broke loose a little, too. Poor Puckett didn't seem to know whom to console. A boy only has two arms. He sort of went around the table hugging each of them a little while before going on to somebody else. His plight struck them all as funny, and they began to laugh while they cried and hugged Puckett. It occurred to Joe then that he'd done the deacon a disservice by not explaining how he felt about ordinary things.

After lunch, Jack and Roy showed up with Mevin's clothes. They approached the house sheepishly, apologizing, and accepting full responsibility for their new friend's condition. Eloise put out some leftovers, and they ate at the table while they told everyone of Mevin's heroic rescue of the white puppy. The brothers were first-rate storytellers, and everybody fell into the tale with the full force of their attention.

As Joe watched and listened, he felt another tear trying to work its way free. But he looked at Ben and thought of his sleepy foot, and decided that this was no time for tears —maybe later, but not now. Ben's gaze broke from the story and met Joe's. He smiled and nodded softly, before looking away. Joe didn't know what that meant, and he never asked Ben about it, but at that moment Joe was as strong as he'd ever been in his life.

෨෮

Later that night after Puckett had gone to bed and Mevin's pulse was checked for the twentieth time, Ben told Eloise that he was going to see a doctor. Earlier, he'd said that he didn't want to worry her and had decided against it. But he did it anyway, not so much because he loved her, but more because he was loved by her. To Ben, love had always been about both truth and protection. It was hard to untangle the two sometimes, but as a man with a family, he understood those parts of love. But Ben was also aware, even if he didn't fully understand it, that there was another part of love. Love was also about letting yourself be loved. The only reason Ben even knew of such a thing was because Eloise had once told him. So that night, Ben loved Eloise by letting her love him.

She cried, of course, and he held her tight. Then she rubbed his sleepy foot for a while and cried some more. There was not a lot talking. Most times that just got in the way. So they just lay there on the edge of a dark night holding on to one another like they'd done for as long as they cared to remember. Granny Catherine's house settled down with creaks and groans, and somewhere amongst the ordinary things sleep took them away together.

A Noah Kind of Direction

Lou Gehrig's disease was more properly known by the name Amyotrophic Lateral Sclerosis, and Joe came to be able to pronounce those words much better than he cared to. It also went by its initials ALS which was much easier to say, but it didn't much matter what it was called. In the end, it all amounted to the same evil thing.

ALS played a pretty fair game of hide-and-seek with the doctors. There was no single test to tell if Ben had it. Every other disease that might have given rise to the same set of symptoms had to be investigated before a definite diagnosis could be made. It was a wicked game. Most of the other diseases were treatable, so everyone hoped that the next test would be positive, indicating that something else was wrong. It was an odd thing, praying for something to be wrong with someone you love, but Mevin, Eloise, and Joe gathered together every day to do just such a thing.

Nothing else was wrong. Ben seemed to know it right off. And after each and every one of the medical tests failed to find an ailment, he worked to comfort the people who loved him the best that he could. And after three months of being tested, poked, x-rayed, and examined, Joe and Mevin babysat Puckett at Joe's house while they waited for Ben and Eloise to get back from their latest appointment.

They came up to the door, quietly but smiling in a kind and peaceful way. Ben and Eloise entered Joe's home without the slightest indication of distress.

"Puckett, buddy, why don't you go on home with your mama. I need to speak with Joe and Mevin for a while."

"Yes sir," Puckett answered, flinging himself off the rocking chair and onto the hardwood floor.

Ben watched his son take his mama's hand and crest the outside doorway. "Puckett," he called. "How about you me and your mama head down to the Mountaineer for some dinner after I finish talking?"

"You bet. Can we get one of those big sundaes?"

"I believe we can."

"All right!" the little boy called, raising his free hand in victory.

Eloise smiled back at Ben, then moved out into the daylight. That left Joe and Mevin staring at the space between them and Ben.

"It's like this, boys," Ben said, reaching to steady the momentum of the rocking chair before taking a seat. "I'm going out a little earlier than I planned on."

The lump grew fast in Joe's throat and the weight of it sat him down on his plaid couch. Mevin stepped toward Ben and leaned down to hug him. They stayed like that for a long while, just hugging onto one another; there were no sobs of grief or cries of pain. They just kind of held on until there was strength enough to let go.

"I need to ask for your help with a couple of things," Ben said, easing away from Mevin and speaking to them both.

Mevin stepped back and sat beside Joe. "Anything," he said.

"The doctor says most folks live three to five years with this sort of thing. Some even live longer. There's some medicine that might slow it down, but it doesn't always work." Ben's words fell out matter-of-fact; not hopeless or resigned, they were just what they were. And they struck with Joe with a purpose that shrank the lump enough for him to speak.

"Any chance of you getting better?" he managed to ask.

"No, Joe. There's no chance of that. I've just got to live with what I have left. And the thing is, what's left is going to gradually get worse. This thing will spread. And my old sleepy foot will sooner or later become my sleepy legs and then arms and then all over. I'll live past my ability to get around. And that's when I'm going need your help. I'd be slow to ask for myself. But…"

"We will be there for Eloise and for Puckett," Mevin interrupted softly. "We will always be there."

"Always." Joe found the voice to agree with his friend on the couch beside him.

"Thank you." Ben exhaled slowly and then rocked easy for a while. "We're not going to tell Puckett, yet. It's hard to know if that's the right thing or not. But we prayed about it." Ben broke into a broad grin and aimed it at Mevin, "And there seems to be a peace in waiting. So we'll wait. And I'd appreciate no crying and carrying on about the whole thing." Ben shifted his grin to Joe, "The boy is bound to pick up on it. And I don't want everybody wallowing around in that kind of business for three years anyway. You're allowed to cry after I'm gone, but let's not grieve over the time that's left. There's no call for it."

"I'll do my best," Joe said.

"That's all a man can ask," Ben replied. "Okay." He stood up. "I've got dinner and a fudge sundae to eat down at the Mountaineer. I appreciate both of you."

Ben took a long stride, then bent down to give Joe the hug that he had left for another day. And Joe tried to soak in some of Ben's strength then so that he wouldn't be a hindrance to him later. After they let go of one another, Joe and Mevin watched Ben limp out the door. As soon as he was gone, Mevin was upon Joe with another hug. In all honesty, Joe knew, that a country music song, or any other type of song for that matter, would not allow for all that sort of man-hugging stuff. Something like that would never sell. But, then again, he figured some things weren't supposed to be sold.

☼☙

Later that evening, bellies were full and bedtime was at hand. Early spring broke boldly during the day but got a little timid after the sun went down. So Puckett crawled under his blankets encased in the warmth of flannel pajamas. Reaching amongst his scattered collection of books on the shelf beside his bed, he withdrew his children's Bible.

"Let's go with this one tonight, Dad."

"All right. What story were you thinking about?"

"You choose."

Closing his eyes, Ben opened the book at random. "Looks like we landed on good old Noah again. Does that suit you?"

"Noah's fine."

The tattered pages of the old children's Bible bore testament to its good use. Ben wasn't sure where it had come from. It could have been his. He sort of remembered having one like it, but most likely it was Eloise's. It'd be like her to draw pleasure from Puckett hearing Bible stories from the same pages she had. However it found its way to Granny Catherine's house, Ben's eyes had lit upon its pages on countless occasions. He figured he'd read the story of Noah's Ark alone at least a couple of hundred times. But on that night, it felt like the very first.

At God's direction, a man short on time worked feverishly to weather a storm and find a safe place for creation's family. Some men called him crazy. Others laughed. The whole thing was silly except to the man and to God. It was a case of beautiful nonsense. And that was the surest sign it was directed by God. After the story was read, Ben knelt beside a sleepy-eyed Puckett and said the now-I-lay-me-prayer in harmony with his son. But when it was done, he lingered a little longer and asked a silent prayer of his own. "Lord, please give me a Noah kind of direction. I'm needing it badly. And I promise to try and follow it the best I know how."

☙☞

"Sold any cows yet, Boy?"

"Not yet, but today seems like the right day for it."

Ben's answer took Joe by surprise, and he paused on it for a while. Then laying his arms across the gate, he moved closer and asked, "Did I hear you right?"

"Yes sir."

"What would, all the sudden, cause you to go and do something like that?"

Ben watched a hawk circle the morning sky and smiled as he spoke, "It's necessary."

"Necessary?"

"Yes sir. Necessary."

Joe rubbed his chin over the response, but let it lie nonetheless. Understanding didn't always happen all at once. It was a shy sort of creature. More often than not, people had to wait on it. Folks who grew too impatient ended up chasing understanding away.

"All right then, I know a man," Joe said.

"A man?"

"That's right, a man who'd be interested in your cows. He's seen them passing by on his way into Kingsport, and more than once he's stopped and asked me if you'd be interested in selling."

"Sounds good."

"Why don't you shoo them over to my side this evening, and I'll get them over toward the back of my place. It's easier to get a trailer in and out of there than it is down on your side. I've already got some grass coming up. They'll be real happy until this old boy picks them up."

"I appreciate you, Joe."

"It shouldn't take but a day or two to complete the whole trade. I'll get you a good deal."

Ben nodded quietly, then watched the hawk go round wider and wider until it simply circled out of sight. "Written any songs yet, Old Man?"

"Not yet."

"Can't spend all your time just figuring on the next good song. What are you going to do when your royalties peter out?"

"I suppose I'll cross that bridge when I come to it."

Ben gave way to easy smile. "I'll be seeing you, Joe."

"Have a good day, Ben."

"Yes sir."

Joe watched Ben for awhile as he made his way to the barn. Ben wasn't limping as bad as he had been. Joe knew better than to take that as any sort of hopeful sign, but he took it as hopeful nonetheless.

༄༅

When Ben showed up for work that day, an immaculate dark blue Dodge pickup sat waiting at the job site. Recognition took a moment to settle upon him and at first he thought it might be an upgrade to Mevin's ancient Datsun. Mevin's pride in the small truck he'd bought after winning his driver's license wasn't large, but Ben couldn't see the lack of it overwhelming his fierce frugality. Nonetheless, there the Dodge sat, towering over the Datsun like a shiny dinosaur. Ben looked at it hard. Then peeling his eyes away, he surveyed the roofline of the newly constructed house he and Mevin were set to roof. Up on top, near the center of the house were two figures already about the business of getting things in order. In the gathering light of morning, the first figure bent and twisted in a way that could only be Mevin. The second stood tall and solid, moving with an even and practiced gate. No doubt about the other figure either, even a blind man could see that Deacon Grainger had come out of retirement.

Ben watched awhile. The two men worked easy together. And he marveled at the sight before the deacon spotted him and climbed down the ladder with the agility of a much younger man.

Ben stepped out from his truck and met the deacon half-way across the brown, grassless yard. "Morning, Mr. Grainger."

"Morning, Ben."

Silence gathered round them like there was nothing else to say. Ben smiled through it and spoke again. "I see you're back on the roof."

"Well, Ben, I know you're sick. And I know that Lou has other things she's attending to. The rest of your crew is unreliable and hasn't come back yet, and that means you're down to just one man, and he has a drinking problem. I figured you might need a steady hand for a little while."

Ben thought about telling the deacon that the work hadn't quite picked up enough for the rest of his crew to come back. And he thought about letting him know that Mevin was the farthest thing from a drunk. But he also thought that the deacon wouldn't be inclined to hear any of it. Some men cut their good in narrow slices, and trying to force them to carve it wider served no true purpose. That didn't make the good any less. It just made it harder to come by. The deacon showed up that morning to do good, and it didn't matter to Ben what blinders came along with it.

"That's mighty kind of you, Mr. Grainger. I wasn't quite sure what I was going to do this spring."

"It'll be only for a short while, mind you. Just until your crew decides to show back up. I can't be expected to shoulder the load forever."

"Oh, yes sir. And I truly appreciate whatever time you can give me."

"No problem, boy."

"Just one more thing, I'm not sure I can afford a man of your experience."

The deacon eyed Ben long and hard. Then, in a voice too soft for a man that large, he said, "This is God's work, Ben. There's no charge for God's work."

Ben found it hard to know what to make of some folks. Just about the time he'd get them figured for one thing, they'd go and do another. And this was never more true than with Deacon Grainger. Maybe it was God's work after all.

The deacon worked like a mule, and he caused Ben and Mevin to work like mules, too. Breaks were for sissies and fifteen minutes was plenty of time for a man to swallow his lunch. Ben and Mevin weren't even able to scratch time enough for their wonderings over baloney and white-bread. There was work to be done, and it needed doing now. Right now.

Afternoon wore into evening, and another day closed itself down without a single injury. The doctors warned Ben that he may begin to experience trips and falls. They said small accidents were bound to beset him as his body gradually lost control of itself. Ben accepted the fate with a smile, but none of it proved more than speculation. Ben became as surefooted as a mountain goat. After a lifetime of torment, pain gathered its bags and moved on to other destinations. Once a job was done, there was no sense in sticking around to gloat over it.

"I'll see you boys tomorrow," the deacon called from the window of his big Dodge. "The days are getting longer, so I say we start a half an hour earlier. We ought to be able to knock this out by the end of the week at the latest." He started the truck rolling and called back as he left, "Half an hour earlier."

Mevin looked at Ben and smiled. "Good Lord, Jesus, and Holy Spirit. That is a man who can work."

"Now you know where Lou gets it from."

Mevin dropped his head at the mention of Lou's name. "Have you heard from her recently?"

"Yes, hold on a minute." Ben strode toward his truck, opened the door, and plucked something from above the visor.

As Ben made his way back, he gave into a longer limp. It always seemed to get worse as the work day wore on.

Extending his arm, Ben handed Lou's latest postcard to Mevin.

The picture was of a nearly naked man sunbathing with nothing on but a sombrero covering his private parts. In a barley legible scrawl, Lou wrote. "Still no boat, but getting closer. Thought the man in the picture was Mister Right, but he's kind of funny about his hat."

Mevin looked at the postcard for a long while and then smiled. "She is a humorous woman. Beautiful and humorous."

"The guy in the picture's not bad, either," Ben said.

"You are a man who is sick in the head," Mevin replied, handing the postcard back to Ben.

"I've heard that before."

Lou sent postcards every few days. Eloise gave them to Ben, and he dutifully carried them to show Mevin. Lou had made it to the Florida Keys, but quickly left for Pensacola and then Jacksonville. She'd even ventured into Mexico for a week or two. Over the three months she'd been gone, it had been tough keeping up with her. Communication flowed just one way. To write her was fruitless. She never called, only sent silly postcards, which Ben and Mevin waited on like kids for Christmas.

"Why don't you come over to supper?" Ben asked.

"I cannot. Claude is bringing his young lady friend to dinner. I must go home and cook."

"Claude has a girlfriend?"

"Yes," Mevin said beaming. "She is a beautiful girl from Atlanta. Claude met her at the University."

"Way to go, Claude."

"Yes. Way to go, Claude."

The two men hugged, a habit they'd unashamedly picked up during the long process of dismissing diseases. Then stepping into their vehicles, they paused together and said, "A half an hour earlier."

Laughter rose light and pure before settling upon the newly constructed house. Cranking their engines, the two men left it there to be gathered up by anyone blessed enough to move in.

☙❦

A Harley lounged in the driveway. Ben killed the truck and stared at it awhile. "Eloise, what in the world have you done?"

Ben coveted Harleys. What man didn't? His savings had stood at nearly the halfway point when Eloise got pregnant, and a young father who goes and buys a Harley ought to be shot. Ben understood this better than most, and he never spoke of his desire to Eloise. But she knew about the savings and that it was spent instead on a small ring and a new baby crib. And she just plain knew Ben. He would put nothing ahead of her and Puckett, but boy, did he like Harleys. Ben considered all this as he watched Puckett exit the house and sprint to the bike, wearing a heavy coat and sporting bare feet. The little boy leapt upon the machine, and within seconds he was racing down the back-roads of his imagination, taking hairpin turns at a hundred miles an hour. Ben laughed out loud and swung his door open.

"I wonder if Noah was ever tempted by a Harley," he said to himself.

The groan of the truck door broke Puckett from his trance and he whirled around on the seat. "Dad!" he yelled, bolting off the back of the bike and racing to his father's open arms. Ben lifted the boy to his shoulder.

"Hey buddy. How was your day?"

"Great."

"I see you've bought yourself a motorcycle."

"A Harley."

"I'm sorry. I see you bought yourself a Harley."

"Come on, Dad. It's not mine. It's Aunt Lou's."

"Aunt Lou's?"

"Yes sir. She's inside. She's come home."

"Thank God." Ben spoke the words with a relief deeper than he realized he'd saved room for. "What do you say we head in the house and tell her howdy?"

Ben set his son down on the hardwood floor and before he could get himself upright again, Lou was in his arms. Well maybe it was the other way around. She squeezed him hard and nearly lifted him past his tiptoes. "Welcome home, Lou," Ben said through a trembling voice. "Welcome home."

Lou didn't speak, just held on tight, giving Ben just enough space to draw a breath or two.

Eloise approached from behind, laid a hand on her husband's back, and spoke for her sister. "Lou's going to be staying with us for a while. We've got her set up in Puckett's room."

Puckett beamed, "I've got me a roommate—a roommate with a Harley."

Lou pulled away from Ben and wiped her face quickly on the sleeve of her flannel shirt. "It's the only kind, honey," she said winking down at Puckett.

Ben reached out and softly took hold of Lou's left hand. "I'm so glad you're here."

"I'll be here for as long as I'm useful, honey. I'm here for as long as I'm needed."

Lou looked a little thinner, and her face glowed red with a fair-skin reaction to the deep southern sun. But other than that, she seemed no worse for wear. Still the same Lou, she cast a long shadow throughout the house. But it was the kind of a shadow that a live oak wore on an overly August day—a place of refuge during a withering afternoon. Lou's presence could not cool the day entirely, but just her being there made it almost tolerable. No-one had called her. Nobody had told her it was time to get back. But like a live oak knows when there's a need to grow its sheltering leaves again, Lou just seemed to know that it was time to come home.

"I'm sorry I haven't been here for... I'm sorry," she said looking Ben in the eyes.

"You're here now, and that's all that matters. That, and the fact that you brought a Harley."

Laughter broke, thankfully, throughout the room. And though Puckett didn't know what was so funny, his giggle leaked out too, which made everybody else a little sad, but not enough to stop the laugher. Ben didn't know whether they were laughing to humble the sadness or to honor it. Maybe they'd just all gone crazy. He decided it didn't matter anyway. It was best to take a laugh however it came along.

৩০০৪

The next day, Ben sold his cows. Joe met him at the gate with the money.

"How did you get this so quick?"

"The old boy I was trading with paid me in advance. He said it might be awhile before he could pick them up."

Ben counted the money and shook his head. "Goodness, Joe, this is a lot."

"Well, the old boy doesn't do a lot of this sort of trading. I've been at it for a little longer," Joe sort of smiled and looked at his feet.

"You didn't cheat anyone, did you Joe?"

"As God as my witness," Joe said looking up and raising his hand for some reason. "It was an honest trade—fair and honest."

Ben pulled a hundred dollars from the stack of bills and lifted it toward Joe. "Broker's fee," he said plainly.

"You got to be joking," Joe replied with a dip of his chin.

Ben broke into a broad smile, "Thanks, Joe."

"Thanks to you too, boy. You've made an old man feel useful. And that's not an easy trick to pull off."

Ben left with the wad of money in his hand without telling Joe his intentions for it. And Joe didn't ask. In East Tennessee, a man's business was his business. They thought that way up North, too, but somehow, the sentiment acquired a kindness in the hills. Joe was glad of it. Because without the kindness, it just meant that folks didn't care.

It didn't take too long to figure out what Ben was doing with the money, anyway. The very next day, after Ben and Lou drove off to work, the bulldozer was delivered.

༄༅

The first day back on the job proved painful, and this time not for Ben. Lou did not speak to Mevin. She could barely bring herself to look at him. Crestfallen, Mevin threw himself into the job and surpassed the intensity of even Deacon Grainger's work.

Mevin knew that Lou had visited the deacon the night she'd returned and let him know that she'd be back at work the next morning, but the deacon showed up undeterred—half an hour early. Some people had a hard time letting go of the good that they intended.

"This is like old times," the deacon roared. "We're making hay with the best of them. And this young fella here is a real worker. I may have misjudged him." The deacon slapped Mevin on the back and laughed.

During the fifteen minutes the deacon allowed for lunch, Mevin asked Ben, "What does the deacon mean, 'misjudged me'?"

"He thinks you're a drunk." Ben smiled.

"Why are you smiling?"

"I think it's funny."

"You think it's funny that the father of the woman I have affection for thinks I am a drunk?"

"Yes."

Mevin shook his head. "It does not matter anyway. Lou's heart is not with me. She cannot even stand to look at me. She does not find me a good man."

Ben choked a little on his baloney and white-bread. "Good Lord, Mevin. The reason she can't stand to look at you is because she doesn't find herself a good woman."

Mevin drew into his own thoughts for what little time was left of the lunch break, then asked, "So why does this make it funny that the deacon believes I am a drunk?"

"I'm not sure. I suppose it's because that's the same thing I've heard said about Noah."

"Noah?"

"Yes, Noah. You know the old boy with the big boat."

"Oh, Noah. I still do not understand."

"You don't have to, right now. You don't have to because I'm still the intermediary. And right now, I'm the only one who needs to understand."

Now Mevin took his turn to smile. "This intermediary, it is quite a challenge, my friend."

Ben sneaked a look at Lou ascending the rungs of the metal ladder. "One of biblical proportions."

"What must I do?"

"You must pray."

Mevin's smile broke larger, and he reached out to his friend, taking him gently by the arm. Then they turned together, slurped down the last of the Dr. Peppers, and climbed back to work.

֍

There was a natural forgetfulness that surrounded Ben's dying, and though everyone on that roof knew he was about the business of it, his dying seemed to escape their minds for long stretches of time. And it was in those stretches that they could let Ben live. Death would come, as it did in every life, but to spend life fretting over death brought nothing but an early frost to fertile ground. So, through the ordinary routine of their work, the folks surrounding Ben were able to keep from asking him to join in their grief. They could let him walk free from the weight of his own mourning. Still, it must have been hard to let someone live when you knew with certainty that they were going to die. It must have been so hard that only the best kind of love could crack it. Up there on that roof was that kind of love. Some of it was more conditional than the rest, but whatever its package, it was still that kind of love.

Ben felt it, and he stood and stretched his body into it. *Thank God*, he thought. *Thank God.*

Lou looked up at him and said, "Daylight's burning, honey. Don't be getting lazy on us."

And Ben smiled broadly and thanked God again.

Making an Ark

The diesel engine cranked early. By the time Joe meandered down to the gate, Roy was cutting deep into the top of the big hill behind Ben's place.

"You figure Roy knows how to work that thing?" Joe asked.

Ben turned from the fence and took a long look across his place. "I believe Roy knows how to work just about anything. And if he can't get something to go the way he wants, he's got Jack to help him out."

"I'd say you're right. Between the two of them, there's not a quandary that can't be outdone."

They stood awhile, and from far away watched Roy work. Jack perched on a large rock to the side of his brother's labor, directing him when needed with hand signals. The sun woke up behind them, and its rays fell upon their effort with a mystical glow. They looked for all the world like angels.

"Thanks, Joe," Ben said, still watching.

"You're welcome, boy," Joe said, and then let curiosity get the better of him, "but thanks for what?"

Ben turned to look at him squarely, "Thanks for not asking what in the wide world of sports Jack and Roy are doing up on that big hill with a bulldozer."

"It's yours to tell," Joe said.

Ben smiled his easy smile. "I'm going to tell you soon. But I've got to get it worked out for myself first. I haven't let on to anyone yet. Even Jack and Roy don't truly know. I'm just going on a feeling right now—a real good feeling."

"Feelings are tough to explain. But if you can gather the right words, they make for the best songs," Joe said, not knowing what else to.

Ben's smile spread wider. "Well, I'm going to have to gather the right words before too long. Folks give you a lot of leeway when they know your time is short. But it's not fair to go too far from normal without laying down some kind of explanation."

Joe eyed Ben for a while in the growing daylight. Ben no longer stood straight, but leaned against a fence post to steady himself. The disease reached up through his legs and began to siphon their strength. He walked slower and soon it was doubtful he would walk at all. But Ben looked happy. He glowed like a lantern full of joy.

"I don't know what you've got brewing up there, Ben," Joe said, nodding toward the big hill. "But the last time I saw you looking like this, it wasn't too long before I was hugging Africans like they were my first cousins."

Ben laughed out loud, plain and strong. It made Joe feel better than he had in a long time. "Thanks, Joe. Thanks."

Ben nodded goodbye and left for his barn, then on to work. Joe watched him hobble along and thought of his "thanks." And this time, he had sense enough not to ask him for an explanation.

੪)ᘓ

Around three weeks later, at lunch time on a Friday, Mevin sat alone on the street curb eating baloney and white-bread. Ben's health treaded both good days and bad, and that particular Friday rolled in bad. So, he had not come to work. The doctors said his disease was progressing faster than usual, if there was such a thing as usual. But Ben stayed outwardly joyous. A purpose seemed to anchor his life, and though he still kept it between himself and God, it was obvious to Mevin that it had something to do with what he was building on the hill. Sitting upon the curb, Mevin considered his friend and lifted a prayer from the side of the street. As it drifted to heaven, he turned and stole another glance at Lou.

"This is ridiculous," he mumbled to himself. "I am a man, not a boy. I can wait no longer in misery. Ben has been cursed by misery, and yet he is filled with happiness. One must labor through his misery before happiness is born. It is time to labor and see if I will give birth."

Mevin couldn't help but smile at the sounds of the thoughts in his head. They did have sort of a rhythm to them, but he'd mastered enough American English to know that setting such thoughts to song was probably not a good idea. It's not that their truth was lacking. It was just that people may tend to get hung up on the thought of a man giving birth. And by the time you had explained that it was a philosophical birth and not a physical one, you would have lost the thread of what you were trying to say in the first place. But then again, maybe he shouldn't sell people short. Hearts, even American hearts, yearned for poetry. Mevin could hear it on the radio and sometimes even see it on television. So maybe, there was a place for words laced with philosophy. Mevin guessed it came down whether a piece of language was beautiful or just ornate.

"When I see him next, I will have to have a wondering with Joe Shelton about this song writing difficulty." Mevin spoke the words aloud to no one in particular.

But, Mevin wasn't truly concerned with putting thoughts to paper and then to song. He was far more interested in just letting them loose from his mouth. The deacon left at lunch for a church meeting. Some of the crew were due back over the next couple of weeks, so it was doubtful that the deacon would work much longer. Lou was back in charge, but she let Mevin assume larger chunks of responsibility. Mevin didn't take it as a compliment. He had convinced himself that it was only because Lou couldn't bring herself to talk to him enough to give orders.

So that afternoon, they found themselves working alone together. "The time is now," Mevin said to himself standing from the curb. "I must try now."

Lou tidied up the lunch mess around her truck and scrambled up the ladder without saying a word. Mevin walked slowly from the street and stood looking up toward the roof. *Now is the time,* he thought, *now is the time.* "Lou, please can you come down the ladder?"

Mevin almost never addressed Lou directly, and it seemed to startle her. "Excuse me, honey."

"Please can you come down the ladder? I wish to speak to you."

"Why don't you come up here?"

"What I have to say... What I have to say," Mevin stuttered slightly, "Must be said on solid ground."

Lou turned from her work and sat. She stared silently at her boots for what seemed like an eternity, but Mevin wasn't moving. He stood stoically at the bottom of the ladder, just waiting on Lou to respond. Finally, for what Mevin guessed may have been the first time in her life, Lou gave in. Sighing deeply, she crested the roof and climbed down the ladder.

"Okay, honey," she spoke softly almost reluctantly, "I'm down here on solid ground."

Mevin said a quick and quiet prayer: "Lord God, Jesus, and Holy Spirit, do not leave me now." Then he swallowed hard and began to speak with a calm clarity he did not think possible in Lou's presence. "Lou, I have a great fondness for you. I do not know how else to describe it. If I were to call it love, I believe that it may frighten you. So I will call it instead by this other name."

Lou stood straight and stock still. She looked up into Mevin's hazel eyes without much expression. She wasn't truly looking, only listening, and Mevin couldn't quite tell what she heard. All he knew was that he had to speak his piece, so on he spoke.

"I do not have much, you know this already. But I have a true heart. I would offer it to you now, but it was given to you a long time ago. I think you know this already as well. I do not know your heart, and I dare not try and interpret your hesitation in finding a fondness for me. I only know that I am weary of not being honest. I think of my country where suspicion and misunderstanding infected the souls of many people and turned them into murderers. I see now my greatest friend dying of a terrible disease. I no longer have the heart for dishonesty. I cannot find a place for it to rest. There is no time for it. So I say these words to you now. In my country, we have two long rainy seasons. One is of greater strength than the other. And when this season comes to an end, there is much joy. A happiness fills the whole of the people. The heart dances, and the soul lifts to heaven. For the first dry days, it is like being in the courtyard of paradise. My life has been a struggle. It has been dreary. But you are the sunshine. You are the end of my rainy season."

Lou's eyes filled to overflowing. More than one teardrop managed to struggle down her cheeks, but she held her gaze sturdy, never once looking away from Mevin. She reached out and took his left hand softly. Then steadying herself, she said, "I've got to go, honey. I'm sorry, but I have got to go." She let his hand drop and walked to her truck without looking back. Rolling away slowly, she left without taking her tools.

ಙಚ

Sunday brought sunshine, and along with the other folks of First Communion Church, Joe congregated to sing, pray, and draw upon the good Lord's strength. And sitting in the back pew, Joe was trying to do just those things as he watched Pastor Lumpkin stride to the pulpit with a noticeable spring in his step.

"Brothers and sisters, I bring you some bittersweet news." The pastor leaned heavily into the pulpit with a grave look upon his red face. "I think it is better to start with the bitter." He dropped his chin to his chest and rested it there for a full minute. Looking up slowly, he continued in a whisper. "This will be my last Sunday as your pastor." He paused there and waited. Joe supposed he expected a collective gasp or emotional outcry of some sort, because the pastor waited for quite a while. Not saying anything, he searched the faces of his congregation, looking for what, Joe was not sure. But the good folks at First Communion grew anxious with his determined silence and began to squirm in their pews. Finally, Pastor Lumpkin let go of a long sigh and continued.

"I can see this makes you anxious, and I don't blame you. I have been your shepherd for lo these many years, and it is hard to let go of a leader. I know, brothers and sisters, I know." Pastor Lumpkin looked to his notes and changed pages. "But take heart. There is not only the bitter, but also the sweet. For in your sacrifice, there is a blessing. I will leave you, but I will go on to larger place, a place with more lost souls, a place where my ministry can touch many more people.

"It is hard for me as well. But I have felt God's call, and He is telling me to go to Chattanooga."

As Joe listened, he tried to have as few un-Christian thoughts as possible. He truly did—he was in church after all. But this was one those times when he struggled. And as he sat on the back pew, he had to admit that he wondered whether the pastor knew the difference between a call and a career advancement. If the pastor wanted a better paying job at a nicer place of work, there was no shame in it. But to claim it as a "call" seemed a little blasphemous to Joe. Joe couldn't profess to know the man's heart, but to be honest, he doubted the pastor's ears would be open to less money in a smaller place. God had made a habit of pulling his best people along.

They almost never wanted to go where He was leading them. Whenever a person couldn't wait to get somewhere, there was a good chance they were headed in the wrong direction. And Pastor Lumpkin couldn't wait to be out the doors of First Communion and down the highway to Chattanooga.

He went on to tell the congregation that he needed to start right away. Such a big church had immediate needs. He arranged for there to be a reception immediately following the service, and after that he and Mrs. Lumpkin would be on their way. The elders of the church had made arrangements for an interim pastor to start next Sunday. He apologized in advance for the quality of the interim, but asked the congregation to understand the difficulty in finding a quality shepherd on such short notice.

৩০০৪

After the foundation set, The Moonshine Brothers took an interest in framing out the structure. They stood together in Eloise's kitchen, looking over the drawings spread out atop the wood-planked table.

"These don't have much in the way of specifics about them," Roy said.

"I know," Ben apologized. "I'm going from some old measures, and I've had to adjust them to keep all the proportions right. This is about as specific as I can get."

"Don't worry," Jack chimed, "We'll be able to figure it out as we go. That's how we go about everything anyway."

"It sure would help though if we knew what we were building."

They looked to Ben who looked back down at the drawings. Jack and Roy followed his gaze, and they all stood and stared for awhile. "It's a boat," Jack said as if finally pushing away all the presumption that clouds a clear picture of the truth.

Roy cocked his head to the left to gather a different angle. "It ain't a boat, Jack. It's an ark."

☼☪

For the next couple of weeks, Lou quit going to work. Maybe, she just couldn't bear seeing Mevin. Or maybe, she figured he couldn't bear seeing her. No matter really, because in the end it still left Mevin all by his lonesome. But like he'd done all his life, Mevin kept at it. He began to reassemble the crew, and like all truly good leaders, he took the lead reluctantly. Some folks might have assumed that a black man in the South would have encountered a fair amount of acrimony in leading a crew of whites, but those folks would have been wrong. Most good working men wanted nothing more than an honest wage, and they'd follow whatever decent path led them there. Color tended to blend toward blindness behind a worthy leader, and Mevin was a worthy leader. The men knew his story. They understood how he came to be there and why it made sense for him to direct them. And, they accepted the situation with a solid nod and the desire to do fine work.

Ben's legs abandoned him. The disease took an especially strong dislike to the lower part of his body, and it ate at his ability to walk or even stand straight. He'd given up the thought of ever climbing atop another roof. Instead, his actions gathered around the building on the hill. At the time, it seemed oddly out of character for Ben to leave Mevin completely to his own devices—not that he would doubt Mevin's ability to carry on, but abandonment was not in Ben's true nature. And to most observers, even to Joe, it looked like abandonment was the hand Ben was dealing. It was understandable and could easily be written off as a consequence of mortality. A man was due to get distracted from life when staring down the barrel of death. But things weren't necessarily what they looked like to observers. And in the deepest part of his heart, Joe knew that true nature should never been written off so easily.

☞☜

Despite Ben's enthusiasm for the building project, he lacked the legs to make it up and down the hill. The folks at the Kingsport ALS support group donated an electric scooter, but it was meant for paved pathways. It had a habit of tipping over every time Ben tried to take it off road. In another place, that might have been the end of things. In most of the world's endeavors, work tended to stop when set apart from its original source of passion. But Jack and Roy had also grown excited, and Ben's lack of legs didn't calm them down in the least.

"Boys," Ben told them, "I'm running down quicker than I thought I would. I don't believe we're going to make it."

"Oh, we'll make it," Roy said flatly. "I ain't worried about that. Are you, Jack?"

"Nope."

"Now that we got that settled," Roy said folding his arms across his chest, "Let's talk about how best to start bending boards."

Ben said nothing for a moment. The brothers would not be argued with, and to try and pay them for their loyalty would be the cruelest kind of insult. Ben seemed to bathe in this stubborn blessing for a while. And when he finally spoke through a gracious smile, all he said was, "Okay."

The building plans grew less and less precise. The figure-it-out-as–you-go project turned more into a make-it-up-as-you-go-along one. That was just fine with the brothers. Their whole life had been that kind of project. But the lack of plans created the need to continually trudge up and down the hill in search of Ben's advice and direction, which left them flushed with a fair amount of frustration. But if it was true that necessity was the mother of invention, then frustration must have been its nursemaid.

"Doggone it, Jack, we've got to figure a way to get Ben up that hill." The brothers sat in the kitchen of the slanted house, waiting on their frozen pizza to bubble.

"I know, but there ain't a whole lot we could do besides carry him or toss him in the wheelbarrow."

"That won't work. I'd rather keep walking up and down that hill than see Ben humiliated. Toss him in a wheelbarrow... you ought to be ashamed of yourself."

"You don't have to fuss at me. I agree with you. I wouldn't want to do anything to humble Ben. But I can't figure what to do. At this rate, he'll leave us before we even get around to building the deck."

The two stared in silence through the pane of cloudy glass embedded in their ancient oven. The dogs caught a whiff of the cooking and went to howling and braying like they smelled the Second Coming, and at that moment the brothers experienced one of those rare instances of simultaneous inspiration. They looked at one another in common understanding and then immediately ran outside.

It took them more than just a little while to round up the bicycle tires and a set of decent axles. And they had to fire up the acetylene torch and the soldering iron. Of course, the proper springs and seat padding had to be fashioned from their large pile of odds and ends, and a braking system had to be designed. It wasn't easy to do, but with skilled hands attached to inspired hearts, a sort of divinity seemed to surround them. And when they finally strung the straps to the harness, they stepped back and found the time spent more than pleasing.

"That about does it," Jack said flatly.

"All except the most important part," Roy cautioned.

"You got any ideas?"

"Well, we designed for three, but we could go five if need be."

"I figure three is enough."

"Then let's pick out three of the most likely and give her a go."

In amongst the mongrel hoard of dogs crowding the front yard, there was a blue-eyed mix named Jake. Jake was more or less a husky, so the brothers chose him to lead. They pondered upon Jake's partners and finally settled on two females by the names of Lucky and Pride. The girls showed no obvious breeding. They were as likely to be one kind of dog as they were another. But they were smart and showed as much "want to" as any dog the brothers had ever owned. The brothers figured that was qualification enough, so they strapped the trio in and proceeded to give it a go.

It was truly a masterpiece. The rolling dogsled was not only functional, but also quite beautiful. Granted, it was a rustic beauty—the kind that gathered around an old grey barn atop a green hill. But that was what passed for beauty in East Tennessee, and given a choice, the brothers would've taken it over the fine-china kind any day. The frame was made of a light planked wood and the fenders fashioned out of scraps off a tin roof to cover the ugliness of the four naked bicycle tires. The sled moved round two independent axles which meant, as long as the dogs behaved, it would turn on a dime. The deep canvas seat sat upon a collection of springs and low in the frame so that Ben would be assured of a smooth ride without having to climb up to get it.

The ingenuity of the contraption was enough to take a person's breath away. But while Jack and Roy operated best with ingenuity, a dog worked better on instinct, and somewhere within old blue-eyed Jake, instinct ran deep. When they strapped the dogs in, Jake took control. Barking and biting at Lucky and Pride, he settled them down then waited on his haunches for the word to go. Roy stepped into the rolling dogsled, took hold of the straps and clicked his tongue like he would with a horse. That was all the encouragement Jake needed. He started out at an even gait, eyeballing Lucky and Pride every so often. Roy let out a good-sized holler, and the sled really got to rolling. Jake understood the signals from the straps and turned when he was told, and Lucky and Pride proved noble enough to follow. Roy rode them around for a good ten minutes, working the dogs and testing the sled.

After gaining sufficient satisfaction, he pulled up beside his brother and said, "That went about as well as a man can expect."

"I can find no place to disagree."

The brothers unfastened their dogs and loved up on them like they were puppies. The dogs lapped up the unbridled affection in the honest way that makes good dogs so likeable. And somewhere within them, the dogs seemed to find a love for the rolling dogsled. From that time on Jake, Lucky and Pride never wandered far from that beautiful contraption. Watching it, protecting it, and waiting on the pure joy of serving it, those dogs were never more than a soft whistle away.

The next day, Jack and Roy rode the sled up to Ben's house, and their whole bodies were smiling.

"Hey, Ben. Come on out here," Jack called from the front porch while Roy giggled from the excitement.

Ben opened the door with a large smile. He supported himself with a metal walker, but stepped from behind it and leaned against the doorframe. "Morning boys. Come on in. Eloise has breakfast cooking."

"Thanks, but no thanks," Jack replied. "We already ate. We're ready to get after it up on that hill."

"Yeah, and you better hurry up and eat, too," Roy chimed in, "You're coming with us today."

Ben's smile flickered, but only for a second. "I'm sorry, boys, but I may be more trouble than I'm worth. I'm not exactly nimble of foot these days."

Roy let go another giggle, and Jack said, "You're not getting out of work that easy." Then they sort of moved to one side, and out of Ben's field of vision, to show him the beauty that was born from frustration. Jake, Lucky and Pride stood at attention next to the beloved contraption almost like they were posing for a picture.

"My Lord," Ben said. "My good Lord."

༄༅

One morning as the sun broke free from hills, Joe looked up toward Ben's building and figured it out for himself. Not just what it was, but what it meant. Joe admitted to being slow. By that time, everybody else could tell it was a big boat. Even Puckett had it figured out. But, besides Jack and Roy, Joe was not sure that anybody else knew just yet that it was also an ark. While they possessed a common appearance, an ark was different than a big boat. An ark did more than just float along on top of the water. It protected from a seemingly endless storm. It got you from an old place to somewhere brand new. It ensured that despite a torrent of tribulation, a family would survive. From the outside, an ark looked a lot like a boat, but Ben wouldn't build just a boat. Ben was an ark builder; he had been his entire life. The fact that he was dying just made it all the more apparent.

༄༅

Not too many days later, Ben took Lou on a rolling dogsled ride. The whole family had about worn those poor dogs out riding and laughing all over Granny Catherine's farm. It was fine to hear such a wellspring of laughter in such a dry time.

Even the hills seemed to drink it up. But Lou resisted climbing aboard the contraption. She claimed she didn't trust it. But Ben figured that it was more likely she didn't trust herself. She'd grown too sad to chance a laugh. Such an obvious sign of happiness would be a heresy to her broken heart.

"Come on and climb aboard, Lou," Ben coaxed.

"No way, honey. I wasn't meant to be dog-propelled."

"But Lou," Ben looked at his sister-in-law with feigned desperation. "I'm dying."

Lou eyed him back, and her shoulders fell. As she struggled to speak, Ben could no longer hold his laugher. At first, he snorted in quick little bursts then bellowed loudly, wiping at his eyes with his shirt sleeve.

"Doggone you," Lou stepped forward and slapped Ben across the side of his head. With his center of gravity teetering upon unsteady legs, Ben dropped like a sack of cement.

"Oh, my Lord," Lou cried. "I'm so sorry, honey. Are you all right? I am so sorry. Are you all right?"

Ben propped himself upon an elbow. His smile stayed wide, but in the corners lived a grimace. "I'm okay. Just give me a minute. I'll be all right in a minute."

Lou sat down beside him and began to sob. Ben had never seen her truly sob before, and he figured it was past time. He let her cry for a while without saying a word. When she began to let up a bit, he said, "Come on and take a ride with me, Lou."

And she whispered, "Okay, honey."

They rode to the top of the hill. By this time the dogs needed little directing, and they came to a stop alongside the ark without being prompted.

"Have you figured out what this is yet?"

"It's obviously a boat, honey."

"It could be."

"Well, it looks just like a boat to me."

"Look out over there," Ben pointed out from the ark and over Granny Catherine's farm. The copper-colored river snaked through a glorious view of an East Tennessee in full green, and then seemed to meander off to the end of the world. "Looks just like we're floating high upon the water, doesn't it?"

Lou paused over the vision before saying, "It does. It truly does."

"It even looks better from those top windows up there. It's sort of what I was going for."

"Well you got it, honey."

"You know why I did it?"

"Because it's a beautiful view."

"No. I mean why I started building this thing."

Lou sighed. "I haven't thought much about it. I know that's funny. All of Mount Carmel is wondering what you're doing. But I figure you've got a reason. And about now, honey, that's good enough for me."

"It's for you." With those words Ben found it impossible to meet Lou's eyes, so he looked at his shoes instead.

"What?"

"I'm building it for you."

"That's crazy. There's no reason for you to build me a boat. A boat?" Lou's breath seemed to catch in her chest. "You're building me a boat. You know I've always wanted a boat, but not here, not a boat on top of a hill. That's crazy. I don't want you to do this for me. I don't know what you think you're doing. Look at me when I'm talking to you."

Ben pulled his head up with a smile. "Are you done?"

"I don't know, honey. I guess it depends on what you have to say next."

"Did I tell you I was dying?"

"Stop saying that. That won't work this time. Now, tell me what it is you think you're doing."

Ben closed his eyes and felt the day. The hills breathed a warm wind, and the whole of existence bathed in it. The moment had come, and he was in it. "Lord," he prayed silently, "Be here with me now."

"What are you doing, honey? Open your eyes and talk to me."

The smile crawled back across Ben's face and he said, "All right Lou, let's talk. I am building this boat for you, at least for you to live in. But I'm also building it for me and for everybody else that I love. Because it may sound crazy, but this boat can be more than a boat if you let it. If you let it, this boat can be an ark."

Lou drew a breath to speak, but Ben raised his hand to shush her. "Let me finish what I'm saying. Then I'll listen to you. But let me finish first, because I'm on a roll now."

Lou tucked her chin while Ben continued. "If you let it, this can be a place of sanctuary. When Eloise starts to miss me, she can walk on up and find a piece of me here. When Puckett needs some instruction on baseball throwing he can knock on the door. And even when old Joe Shelton needs some inspiration for the next song he's never going to write, he can come to this place to find some conversation. Now, I know it's a lot to ask, but I'm asking anyway. You're strong. You've always been strong, and you can do it. I know you can. But I don't want you to do it alone.

"There are times when it is right to withhold your own happiness. The reasons for doing that are as long as your arm. But now is not the time, and there are no truly good reasons. You and I both know that your happiness on this earth is all wrapped up in Mevin. And I'm asking you right now to make us both happy. I'm asking you, with the help of the good Lord, to give in to your love for Mevin and make this boat an ark."

A Likable Truth

Joe watched from the back pew of First Communion Church as the fidgety man stood above the gathering. Between the smooth, pale face and green eyes, it was tough to get a read on exactly how old he was. It didn't make much difference anyway. No matter his actual age, the people of First Communion would take one look at the man-child in the front of the church and think of a single word: "young". At first, Joe thought he was somebody's son playing the fool. He half expected his mama to come up and grab the young man by the ear, but the young man kept standing there, nervously waiting for the muted hum over his unfortunately youthful appearance to subside.

When he did finally speak, his voice cracked. And honestly, Joe wasn't sure whether it was because of his nervousness or lack of physical development. Nonetheless, he did speak. And when he did, it went to show that the nature of someone's words were more important than how they sounded coming out.

"Excuse me," he said, calming the last few whispers among the congregants. "My name is Sam Haley, and at least for a little while, I'm your new pastor." The young man took a long look down upon the congregation and continued. "If you don't mind, I'd like to come out from behind this pulpit. I've never been that comfortable being back behind of one of these things." No one responded, and the young man seemed to take that as a sign that nobody minded. He stepped down from the pulpit and planted himself eye-level with his congregation, but only for a moment, because a young man fashioned with such a wiry frame could not hold still for long. So, he began to walk up the center aisle. And as he did, he spoke. His voice was still squeaky, but not soft or mumbly. Even from the far back corner of the church, Joe could hear him clearly.

"I would guess a lot of you are looking at me and shaking your heads, at least on the inside. I think I would if I were you. I am young, I know, and a young pastor has a lot to learn. But I'm not quite as young as I look, and as it clearly states in the Gospel of John, "It's not the years, it's the mileage."

The congregation appreciated the attempt at humor and let go of a soft chuckle. But the young man's voice found no confidence in the breakthrough. In fact, it seemed to tighten even further.

"Still, I am younger than you would probably like. But I'll tell you now that being young is not the worst thing about me. I found Jesus Christ in a rehab center seven years ago. I have never been married, because, quite honestly, I have not been what you would call a great catch for a woman. Come to think of it, I'm not what you would call a great catch for a congregation, either. You needed a pastor on short notice. I am what you get on short notice."

The congregation fell completely silent. The blatant humility of the young man drew them to his words in a way that the polished feel of a practiced sermon never could.

"I realize that I am an interim. The elders will continue to look for a permanent replacement for Pastor Lumpkin. I don't blame them. Given their shoes, I'd walk in the same direction. But I must tell you that I want to be here. I want to be here as long as you and God are willing to have me here. This is a nice place, and I've spent far too much of my life in places that were not. My hope is that I will stay here as your pastor for a good long while. I'm sorry to say that the truth about my past is not pretty. But the more God is in a person's life, the less the truth is an adversary. And through the redeeming power of Jesus Christ, I have come to a likable truth."

Likable truth—now there was a phrase worth remembering. Joe found himself trying to rhyme the word "truth" with something other than "youth". "Proof" might have been good. But the young man's words drew Joe back from the thoughts of his own.

"I am far more the sheep than the shepherd. I know that is a funny thing for a pastor to say. But the wolf has beaten me too many times to claim otherwise. So for the time I am here, I'll have to be more a part of the flock than any sort of leader over it. I'm sorry, but God hasn't given me any other way to go about it."

Joe glanced over the congregation and, as usual, found Ben smiling. He sat in his wheelchair near the red exit doors of the church. Puckett leaned against him and their eyes shone together as they listened to the young man speak. Joe could not help but be infected by their joyous fascination, and he found himself sharing it with them. As the young man talked on, Joe became enamored with his honest confession of repentance and his open declaration of a faith built upon a foundation of fault and failure. And as he looked around the sanctuary, it dawned on Joe that everyone had some sort of pain. Somewhere, each and every soul hurt. The thought of it suddenly made the behavior of more than a few individuals a little easier for him to take. For the first time, Joe truly understood why God was so insistent about loving your neighbor.

"Well, that's enough about me. We'll get to know each other better over the next little while. I hope to start making home visits next week. And, if you would like, we can talk longer then. In the meantime, please turn in your Bibles to Matthew 5:14."

☙◊❧

Joe sat still in the rocker, just thinking and constructing how this particular story could be told. It was not his story, but he would tell it, because otherwise it might not be told at all. No matter how beautiful, those involved were just too private to tell it themselves. It was just not their way. But, it was Joe's way. He'd told a story or two in his time and though most had been through lyric and song, he had an ability for speaking a sturdy tale as well. So, he was fairly certain that the tale needed telling and that he was the best suited to do it. First, it would be to Puckett and then who knows. Joe started the chair rocking and his mind eased into its rhythm while it continued to craft.

Joe wasn't there of course. Neither one must have felt the need to invite old Joe Shelton along. But, Joe did know that the proposal came on that first date. He supposed it wasn't the first time in the history of romance that such a thing happened, but most certainly it was one of the few times that it actually made sense. Joe didn't know what transpired on that date, or how it ended, or even if there was a kiss. Nobody felt the need to tell him, and he had sense enough not to ask. Some things, especially romantic things, had the license to remain private, even from the speculation of a storyteller. But the reason for the answer to the proposal was different. Though they hadn't felt the need to tell Joe about that either, the reason she answered the way she did begged for a little creative conjecture.

Lou said "yes." After running away and fighting against it, she said "yes" to the date that Ben arranged. Then, when Mevin, fearing that this would be his one and only shot, asked for her hand in marriage, she said "yes" again. Just like that. "Yes." There wasn't any hemming or hawing or putting it off. She looked the man that she loved right in the eyes and told him "yes."

The best storytellers cautioned their understudies against a sudden change in a character's heart. In real life, people were ill-suited for epiphany. They were just not likely to change all of the sudden. In real life, the stability of a closed heart was often more appealing than the risk of an open one. And as they should be, most good storytellers were true in their devotion to real life. So, sudden changes were best left to frogs and princes. But sometimes revelation sort of snuck up on you. Sometimes, after years of hard work, a person became an overnight success. Sometimes, even in real life, dawn broke with the same old sun and same old sky, but for some reason a person recognized it as a brand new day. And Joe figured after hearing Ben out and finally giving a good listen to her own heart, that's exactly what happened to Lou. Joe hoped they wouldn't kick him out of the good-storytellers club for saying so.

৪০৬৪

Pastor Lumpkin required several weeks of pre-marital counseling before allowing a wedding in his church; so that nobody could argue with him, he even had it written into the bylaws. During the time of counseling, Pastor Lumpkin would most likely have strongly discouraged an interracial union, maybe even backed it up with some well-pruned scripture. Marriage asked a hard road sometimes, and being of mixed race only added to the burden. Pastor Lumpkin probably would have emphasized that point heavily. But Pastor Lumpkin wasn't at First Communion anymore. Sam Haley was.

"So you want to get married?" he asked, sitting on a small wooden chair behind a card table in Pastor Lumpkin's emptied-out office.

"Yes, honey. We want to get married."

"In this church?" The young pastor rubbed his smooth chin roughly.

"Is there an issue with us being married? We are both Christian. We have not yet consummated our union or done anything to defile our union's purity." Mevin spoke with an earnest hope in his church.

The young pastor stopped rubbing his chin and smiled through his fingers. Mevin looked from the pastor to Lou, who wore the "you're an idiot" look perfected by women with husbands all over the world. Mevin bowed his head slightly and turned back to the young pastor. "Is there an issue with us being married in this church?" he continued in soft voice.

"Quite possibly," the young pastor said, while scratching the inside of his ear with an index finger.

"And that would be?" Lou asked evenly.

"Pre-marital counseling."

"Pre-martial counseling?"

"Yes. The bylaws of the church state that all couples must go through pre-marital counseling by the pastor before they are married in this church."

"We are willing to do this," Mevin said smiling.

"You are?"

"Yes, honey, we are."

"With me?"

"You are the pastor."

"I know, but won't you feel silly getting pre-marital counseling from me? I mean, what do I know about it?"

Lou let go a laugh. It was the first good laugh she'd released in a long time. "I like you, Pastor Haley, honey. I can already tell that I'm going to like you better than any other preacher I can think of. And I appreciate your honesty. But you are the pastor, and this church has bylaws, so you need to start counseling."

Mevin broke into a wide grin. "I am also prepared to be counseled."

The young pastor again rubbed his chin and fidgeted in his seat. "All right then. Let's do some counseling. Mevin, why do you want to marry this woman?"

"She is my destiny."

"That's nice. That's truly beautiful. Okay then, Lou, why do you want to marry this man?"

"Because I am his destiny."

"Okay. That's nice, too. Not all that original, and sort of self-centered, but I suppose it will do."

It was too much. Mevin started to chuckle, and Lou broke into the girlish giggle that was so at odds with her natural demeanor. The young pastor joined their laughter with dancing eyes and a hearty chuckle of his own.

"Very good. I don't know much about it, but I've heard that a sense of humor is very important to a good and lasting marriage. A sense of humor allows the soul to exhale. It's the most underused antidote in all of God's creation. I know your family has a heavy weight, and I suppose, being of different skin colors may add some weight to your marriage as well. A sense of humor will help give Jesus a way to lighten the burden."

Mevin and Lou sat silent, allowing the words of the young pastor to sift toward their hearts.

"Okay, that's about it."

"That is it? That is all of our counseling?" Mevin smiled broadly at the young pastor.

"That can't be it, honey. We're going to need a little more than just that."

"Yeah, it does seem that there should be more. I think we have to fill up at least three weeks. Okay. How about this? For the next two weeks, I want you to read at least one passage from a King James version of the Bible on love, fidelity, or marriage every night together, out loud. Then for one week, pray out loud together about your hopes and fears around combining your two lives into one. After that, we will have successfully fulfilled our obligation on pre-marital counseling, and you can be married in First Communion Church in accordance with the bylaws."

Lou stood up, leaned over the card table, and hugged the pastor with such strength that there was an audible pop in his back. "Honey, you are so precious. I'm glad that you will be marrying us."

Mevin reached over and patted the red-faced pastor on his shoulder. "Very good. You are a very good man. A wise man. A man worthy of being a pastor."

☙☙

"It's all right to cry, sweetheart."

"No it's not. There'll be time for crying later. We agreed that there would be no tears until later. I'm sorry. I'm so sorry that I'm crying." Eloise sobbed with a heaviness that Ben knew she usually saved for the times he was up at the ark with Jack and Roy. But that morning the weight must have come upon her suddenly, and she just couldn't hold up under it.

Ben watched her from the green winged-back chair in the family room. He wanted to go to her, to hold her, to wrap his arms around her, but his legs were unwilling. He couldn't stand up on his own anymore. So he spoke to her. Through shallow breath, he rallied a clear comforting voice.

"It's all right to cry. There's nothing wrong with a few tears now and then."

She came to him. Sitting on the arm of the green winged-back chair, she leaned into him and kissed his cheek. "How in the world can Ben Bellamy be dying? I mean that is utterly ridiculous."

"Everybody dies, Eloise."

"I know. But you're not supposed to, not yet. If you were supposed to die young, you should have died a long time ago. How many accidents have you survived in your life?" She began to sob again, but Ben could not help smiling.

"I guess I have had an accident or two haven't I?"

Eloise didn't respond.

"It's going to be all right. I'm sorry that I'm leaving. But everything's still going to be all right."

"How can you say that?" Eloise managed to say.

"Because it has to be, Eloise. Some way, somehow, it just has to be. Otherwise, it wouldn't make any sense."

"It *doesn't* make any sense."

"Oh yes, it does. We just don't know enough to make sense of it. But I will soon. Soon, I believe, I'll know enough. I'd like to tell you when I do, but I don't believe the post office picks up letters from the afterlife." The smile rose again upon Ben's face.

Eloise gathered in her sobs. "Aren't you scared?"

"A little. I'm scared a little. Mostly, though, I think I'll be relieved. I can't throw a baseball with Puckett. I can't snuggle with you at night. Sometimes, I have trouble even drawing the next breath. It's getting tough to wring some joy out of each day. So it's time to go. It's time for you and Puckett to be sad for a while then work your way back to being happy. And if I stay around too long, I'm afraid you'll forget how to do that. I'm struggling to be a good husband to you, and whatever chance I had at being a good father to Puckett is growing slimmer by the day. So I'm not anxious to get there, but I'll be ready when I do."

Eloise squeezed herself down into the green winged-back chair and got as close to Ben as physically possible. "I love you," she said. "I love you so much it hurts."

೮೦೧

The wedding stayed small. It tried to grow big, as weddings typically do, but Lou willed it into intimacy. In the end, only a few dozen smiling faces gathered in the First Communion sanctuary, and Joe was more than honored that he was one of them. Claude came up from his new job in Atlanta to stand beside his brother as best man. Before the ceremony, he went to Lou, and holding her tightly against a finely made suit, he whispered. "You have found the best man in the world. Love him for me and for my mother and father. I have not loved him as I should, and they could only love him for a short time. Love him for us all. Love him as he deserves."

Ben gave Lou away. The center aisle of First Communion was too narrow to walk beside a wheelchair. So, Lou hiked her bridal gown up and pushed her escort to the front of the church. She parked Ben a little past the front row and bent down to kiss his smiling face.

"I love you, honey," she said.

"I love you, too," he replied.

Puckett stood next to Claude as Mevin's groomsman. Joe had the honor of standing beside Puckett. On the other side, Eloise stood beside her sister and Miss Emma looked ravishing standing beside Eloise. Jack and Roy sat beaming from the third pew. Behind them, Mr. Unsler looked like he could barely contain himself. Far in the back sat Dr. Schilling, and Joe got the feeling that the doctor wished he was Mevin that day.

While the well-polished faces sat quietly waiting for the ceremony to begin, Joe looked once more for Deacon Grainger, but there was no call to. He wasn't coming. When Lou told the deacon about her plans to marry, he apparently mumbled something about in-grafted branches and refused to discuss it further. So for the second time, he sat in his neatly trimmed home while one of his daughters took her shot at happiness. Joe admitted to himself that the thought of it all lit a little anger in his belly. Most times, happiness wasn't tidy. True joy was bound to be a little messy. For the life of him, Joe couldn't figure out why a man blessed with such wonderful daughters hadn't come to realize that. He wasn't a bad man, just one who struggled to find a balance between the command of law and the commission of love. The thought of all that made Joe a little sad. He couldn't claim to be a Bible scholar, but the little he did know about Jesus told him that the law didn't hold a candle to the love. And he wondered why a man as well-versed in the Bible as Deacon Grainger hadn't come to know that, in the end, it was a book about love. Joe hoped then, that one day while in the midst of memorizing another verse of scripture, the deacon might just take a breath and realize that love was the reason for the words. Joe figured that if he could just come to know that one simple truth, he could keep both his tidy house and his family.

Joe didn't think the chance of that kind of revelation held much promise. After all, it had taken years before the deacon even darkened the door of his grandson's life. But that was what hope was for. Hope made no promise. It just made hope.

When the young pastor pronounced Mevin and Lou man and wife, the small crowd cheered. The hoots and hollers mixed with applause and bounced off the rafters and back down to the pews. It made it seem as if more people than just those in the church were cheering the unlikely pair. And Joe held no doubt that they were.

༄༅

Jack and Roy didn't seem pleased, but they allowed it nonetheless and after the ceremony, everyone moved from the church to the ark. Inside were finger sandwiches and wedding cake, and as the small crowd gathered for a blessing, the brothers whispered and pointed at all the rough edges that needed smoothing. Jack and Roy worked with enthusiasm, but they hadn't completed the task to their own satisfaction by the wedding day. Everybody else, though, recognized the gifted craftsmanship that gave birth to the structure before them.

There were no rooms on the bottom, only windows and open space. Polished wooden planks ran in bent patterns to form the walls. The kitchen rambled along one side, and the only inside door was to a small bathroom. An open staircase climbed to a loft with three rooms and more windows. A hatch opened to the roof, or better said to the top deck, where the boys had designed a large stone patio. From the patio, it seemed as if you could see all of East Tennessee. The whole of it was magnificent—a divine structure built with humble hands.

"Lord almighty, bless this house. Make this house a home where the weary come to rest and the poor in spirit find safe passage. Jesus Christ hold this home close to your heart, and let its inhabitants open their own hearts to your will and guidance. Holy Spirit find in this home a dwelling place for your graciousness and hospitality. Protect those within its walls, and give them peace." The pastor let his words lay silent for a moment and then continued, "Thank you Lord for the food before us. Please bless it to the nourishment of our bodies and our souls to your service. Amen."

"Amen," the crowd agreed and everyone began to eat and wander around.

೫೦ಌ

Later that night, Ben's breathing took an especially shallow turn. He gulped at the air around him, trying to find enough to stay conscious. He fought hard and, that time, he won, but it left him shaken, not because he was worried about dying, but more because he was worried about finishing.

Early the next morning, Ben hauled himself into the rolling dogsled. It'd been a while since he'd been able to do it on his own. Jack and Roy hitched up Jake, Lucky, and Pride every morning before heading off to the ark, then Eloise usually helped Ben get saddled up in the contraption if he was able to go at all. But on that early morning, he found his own strength, or maybe it was given to him.

Jack and Roy were on the starboard side hammering on something, possibly each other, while Mevin worked on a flower bed out front.

"Good morning, Mevin," Ben said, bringing the dogs to a stop. "You look very married this morning."

"Good morning, my friend. You look very good yourself."

"You are a bad liar."

Mevin looked toward the ground and then stepped toward his friend. "What gets you out so early, Ben?"

"I have a question for you."

"I will try and answer well."

"Puckett…" Ben stopped to gather his voice. "Puckett…" He tried again, but other words would not follow that name. "I need…" He let go of a soft whimper and closed his eyes for a long while. "I need you to be my intermediary."

Mevin stepped closer, then as though sensing it was not a time for physical closeness, he stopped between the dogs and the flower bed and said, "It is my truest blessing to be your intermediary."

"Thank you," Ben said coaxing the dogs to turn around. "Thank you."

"Ben," Mevin called as the rolling dogsled started back down the hill.

"Yes, Mevin."

"My father… he will be waiting for you. Tell him I love him. And my mother… she will be with him. Tell her so as well."

A broad smile broke across Ben's face, "I will Mevin. I'm looking forward to it."

The morning shook itself loose from the hills and its light fell through the window and upon Puckett's small bed. He awoke to find his father watching him from the motorized scooter.

"Good morning, buddy. How did you sleep?"

"Pretty darn good. How 'bout you?"

"Not so well, and that's part of the reason I wanted to catch you before you got good and going today."

Puckett rubbed his eyes and said, "I've got to go to the bathroom."

"Go on, then. I'll be here when you get back."

By the time Puckett took care of his business, Ben was sprawled out on top of the bed. Puckett snuggled in next to him and said, "I'm ready."

"Ready for what?"

"You want to talk don't you?"

"I suppose I do."

The two of them lay there for a while, just staring at the ceiling and listening to each others heartbeats. There was no good time for bad news, but Ben figured the morning to be the best bad time. A person ought to do what needed to be done right off the bat, before the mind got cluttered with all sorts of less important matters and before the day grew too long. As the hours passed, "putting it off until tomorrow" made more and more sense. But tomorrow was more of a gift than a given. It was under no obligation to come. So it was best to speak bad news in the morning. The same was true for saying prayers.

Still, Ben found it hard to muster the words that would break his son's heart. "Puckett, you know I've been pretty sick."

"Yes sir."

"Well, I have to tell you that this isn't the sort of sickness that you can get better from."

"Yes sir."

"This is the sort of sickness that takes you off to heaven sooner than you might otherwise want to go."

"Yes sir."

"Do you understand what I'm trying to say?"

"Yes sir."

"Well, so I know that you know, can you tell me what you're hearing?"

Puckett stayed quiet for a while. Ben heard him sniffle and felt the boy tremble just a bit.

He snuggled closer to his father and in a thin, little voice he spoke the words that Ben couldn't quite get around to. "I'm hearing that you're going to die."

"That's right."

"Does Mom know?"

Ben couldn't help but smile at the question, "Yeah, she knows."

"How long until?"

"Not very."

"I'm going to miss you, Daddy."

"I'm going to miss you, too, buddy."

They cried together on that bed for a good long time. It wasn't the blubbering-I-can't-catch-my-breath kind of cry. It was more of an easy cleansing sort of cry—long on tears and short on words. At its end, Ben had one thing left to say.

"When I'm gone, you be good to your mama. You listen to her and do right things. Also, I want you to listen to Mevin. You spend all the time you can with him. I've talked to him already, and he wants you to be with him as much as you can. He is a good man. Try and be like him. He knows what a good father does, and he will be good to you."

That set the tears off again, but only for a little while. After the crying stopped, they lay again in silence until Puckett's hunger broke it.

"How 'bout some French Toast, Dad?"

"Sounds like a good way to start the day."

After the dishes were clean and the table wiped free of stray syrup, Puckett headed outside, leaving his parents in the kitchen.

"You talked to him, didn't you?" Eloise asked.

"Yeah, we talked. He asked me if you knew. I told him you did, but I'm not so sure."

"What in the world are you talking about?"

"Listen Eloise, there's something I need to say."

"You better not."

"Better not what?"

"You better not tell me to find someone else after you're gone, to go on with my life, or whatever other foolishness you're about to say."

"Eloise."

"No. I don't want to hear it."

"Eloise you're so young. It'd break my heart to think of you being lonely, without anyone to sit on the porch swing with. You've got to promise me that you'll at least try."

Eloise dropped her chin to her chest, then lifted it high and spoke. "Okay then, I'll promise you. I'll promise that just as soon as I find someone that is as good and honorable and kind as you, I'll try. I'll promise that just as soon as I find someone whose own well-being is never a consideration, I'll try. And I promise, just as soon as I find someone who makes me feel the kind of joy that they only talk about in storybooks, I'll try. Until then, I'll just wait to see you again."

The kitchen filled up with silence and all the world seemed to center its attention around the sound of the dripping faucet.

"How about handsome?" Ben finally asked.

"What?"

"Your next boyfriend. He doesn't have to be handsome like me?"

Eloise smiled through the tears gathering within her eyes. "I like them big, clumsy, and ugly. You ought to know that."

She came to him and pressed his head to her chest. And all Ben could feel was grateful. He'd lived on borrowed time, but he'd spent it wisely. And now all that was left to do was find its end.

A Necessary Song

About four weeks later, Eloise called Joe. "He's been asking after you, Joe. He'd like to see you."

Joe decided to walk. Fall had settled in among the hardwood trees and usually he would have fired up the truck for the ride down, but Joe could walk, so he did. Along the way, he picked up a piece of fence, just a little strand of wire really. It had come loose from around the gate. And it was silly, Joe knew. But since Ben couldn't come to the gate, Joe wanted to bring the gate to him, or at least a piece of it. It wasn't even the gate itself, just an old scrap of wire. Joe got to the door and almost tossed it away. But he couldn't, so he didn't.

"Howdy there, Ben, how in the world are you?" Joe tried to sound cheerful, but it came out silly. He was infected with some kind of silliness, and he silently cursed it.

Ben smiled, "Not so good, Joe." His voice was raspy, and he was drawing shallow breaths. "How about you?"

"Well me, I'm all right, I guess." Joe just couldn't stop sounding silly.

"What's that you're fiddling with?"

"Oh, this? This is just an old piece of barbed-wire. I found it near the gate. I suppose I figured I'd bring it along because… oh, never mind."

Ben laid a quiet look upon Joe and then said, "Thanks Joe, Thank you so much. Do you mind if I keep it?" Joe could've sworn Ben was close to crying.

"Oh sure. Here you go." Joe held it out like Ben somehow had the ability to take hold of it. And when it finally dawned on Joe that Ben's arms had stopped working, he stepped around the bed and laid the old piece of wire on the night table.

"I'm going to miss you, Joe."

"I'm going to miss you too, boy."

"Eloise and Puckett…"

"I will take care of them like they were my own."

"I know. I know you will. But there's something else. Eloise got a job as a teacher's aide in Kingsport. And she has this idea that she may want to become a full-fledged teacher someday. But she's got to go to college for that and she's unsure of herself. When I'm gone, please help her see how good and smart she is. Please don't let her think low of herself. Please do for her the sort of big things you've always done for me."

"Why, Ben, you know I will. But I can't honestly say that I've ever done much big for you."

Ben let go of a weak laugh. "Joe, you showed up at the gate every day. Every single day. I'd say that's as big a thing as anyone has ever done for me."

Joe didn't know what to say. Imagine that, he thought, a songwriter at a loss for words. So, he stood there like a silly dummy, just looking at this man who somehow attributed a piece of his unwavering decency to him. After a while, Ben's eyes fluttered and then all of the sudden just closed. Joe watched for the rise and fall of his breathing and determined that he'd just drifted off to sleep. So Joe left. Without another word, he made his way home.

ೞಚ

Ben died within the month. Joe wished to his soul that he could've found a way to make his death sound poetic. But it wasn't, so he couldn't. ALS took him and he died hard. The doctor said he went much quicker than most, and there wasn't a lot poetic about that. Death came when it did, and sometimes no matter how hard a person tried, he just couldn't find a reason or a rhyme.

The funeral was well-attended, and Pastor Haley equipped himself ably.

"There are those who will tell you that this is not a time for sorrow, but one of celebration. And I wish I could say that, but I can't. A good life is no longer, and it seems to me that makes it a good reason to cry. So let's cry and let's pray. Let's open our despair to the healing power of the Holy Spirit and let's commend Ben Bellamy to everlasting life. And then perhaps, at some other hour, we'll be able to celebrate. At some later hour, we'll gather with smiles and old stories. But this morning the Lord won't begrudge us some time to mourn. Knowing what I do of Ben, I suppose the Lord would like a little time for that as well."

The mourners filed out of the church and then collected again for the graveside service. When it was over, they went their separate ways. Joe went home and cried. He figured the others did the same.

That evening, family and friends gathered again at the ark. Lou served them from donated casserole dishes and plates full of reheated fried chicken. Laughter found a place to bloom, and they told some stories. But leaving that evening, the realization that it was time to try to go on without the best person any of them had ever known seemed to hit them all hard. And one by one, the mourners staggered out from the ark and into the night.

The next day, Joe brought the cows back. He'd never sold them to anybody. The whole time, he had them hidden on the lower side of his place. It was dishonest, but it was a decent sort of dishonesty. Joe couldn't say that he felt bad about it. He knocked on the door and asked Eloise if he could speak to Puckett.

She looked past him at the herd and smiled. "Thank you, Joe. You are a good man."

"It's just a few cows."

"No it's not, you old goofball. It's a lot more. Just like that piece of fence was a lot more."

"Ben told you about that silliness?"

"Yes, he told me about it. And he also asked to be buried with it. With so much going on, I forgot to tell you, but he was buried with that piece of barbed-wire. I don't think that's silly at all."

Joe had to sit down. So he sat. Right on the front steps, he plopped himself down and teared up again. Maybe silliness was not such a sin after all.

Eloise sort of rubbed Joe's head and said, "I'll go get Puckett."

Shortly, the boy popped from the front door and sat down beside Joe.

"How you doing, Puckett?"

"I'm making it. How about you? You don't look so good."

"Oh, I'm okay. I'll be all right in a minute. I brought your cows back." Joe nodded toward the herd.

"My cows?"

"Yes sir, your cows. They were your great-granny Catherine's and then your Daddy's. So, I'd say that you're now the rightful owner."

"You think?"

"Yes sir, I think. And if you want me to, I'll help you take care of them until you grow big enough to do it on your own."

Right then, the most amazing thing happened. Without saying a word, Puckett climbed into Joe's lap and hugged his neck with everything the little boy had. In the whole of Joe's life, he'd never felt so necessary.

༂༅༄

Days turned to weeks and weeks crowded into months, and months, well, they kept collecting toward a year—all of which colored more of Joe's hair to gray. Down at the gate, it took a while for Mevin and Joe to find a harmony to their talking. But earnest voices had a way of making do. The silence gradually lost its hold, and conversation became honest and easy.

"It is over."

"With Jack and Roy, you mean."

"Yes. They have finally accepted the gift."

Before Ben had passed, he and Eloise had a lawyer draw up some papers giving Jack and Roy a few acres of their land upon Ben's death. It was a small gesture, but the brothers had a tough time accepting even a little kindness. Joe figured that they weren't used to being appreciated. It took a long time to convince them to take the gift, and in the end Eloise had to cry to get them to sign off on it. Instead of just a few acres, it was as if the boys thought they were inheriting a whole new world. And in a way, Joe supposed that they were.

"How's school coming?"

"Good. For Puckett, he is a smart boy and very good to his classmates." Mevin beamed with an honest pride. "And Lou says that school for Eloise is good as well."

"That's great. I'll say something to both of them about it. Puckett ought to be tearing up on that dogsled before sun gets much past those hardwoods, and Eloise is taking pity on an old man and feeding me tonight."

"Very good."

"How about you, young friend? Are you figuring on any children yet?" Joe couldn't hide his grin. "A man with a thriving business needs somebody to leave it to."

"No, no plans. I am fortunate to have an heir already. But how about you, old friend? Have you written any new songs? A man must not rest only on what he has done before." Mevin's smile came freely.

"No, nothing new. I haven't done anything new in a long time."

"Maybe it is time." Mevin's smile receded. "This..." he said sweeping his arm across Granny Catherine's farm, along the river, past the slanted house of Jack and Roy, and on up to the ark on the hill, "Is this not a necessary song?"

When they parted in the morning, they always hugged goodbye—even early on when they had little to say. It should've seemed odd, a tall African man hugging an old hillbilly. But it didn't seem that way at all. It just seemed natural.

As was Joe's habit, he went to the barn to putter around while he waited for Puckett. And in amongst his shifting and straightening, a tune started tickling the inside of his head. It was rough. But it was real, and it was pleasing. And Joe sort of smiled at it, but then quickly dismissed it in favor of directing his attention toward a loose board on one of the interior doors. Reaching into his nail can, he drew out a three or four "10 pennies" and plunged them deep into the pocket of his dungarees.

"Now where did I lay that hammer," he mumbled before sighting it on the far shelf.

After retrieving the hammer, Joe was finally ready and he steadied the loose board with his elbow while he reached back into his pocket for a nail.

"What in the world," Joe said as he placed the nail to the board.

Halfway up the "10 penny" was a piece of wrinkled paper. *It must have pierced it in my pocket,* Joe thought. And he almost hammered in anyway. But the lack of symmetry made Joe stop. He didn't want some ragged piece of paper messing up a perfectly driven nail. So Joe released the loose board, put the hammer down and slid the paper off the end of the nail. Then he opened it. More out of curiosity than anything else, he just wondered what had been hiding in his pocket for so long.

It was an old grocery store receipt, and it must have been through the wash at least a few dozen times. It was faded and soft to the point of crumbling, but the depth of the pocket had protected it some, and it was still obvious what it was. And when Joe turned it over, he found the two words he knew would be there.

And the tune started tickling the inside of his head again, this time with a little more clarity. And he got to thinking about some boys he still knew up in Bristol, who could help him put a finish on it. Then he got to thinking that maybe Mevin was right. Maybe this was a necessary song. And just maybe, it was about time that he wrote it.

The End

Author Bio

In his seven years as a newspaper columnist, Jeff McCord estimates that he has published somewhere in the neighborhood of two hundred columns. He started out writing for "The Rogersville Review"—Tennessee's oldest active newspaper and along with his wife currently writes a column for the "Kingsport Times-News." McCord published his first essay, "Manhood and Kaptain Kangaroo" in 1994 and has been publishing essays and short stories ever since. A native of Sandy Springs, Georgia, Jeff McCord now resides in Kingsport, Tennessee with his wife and three children. *Awkward Grace* is Jeff McCord's debut novel.

Order Form

If not available from your local bookstore or favorite online bookstore, send this coupon and a check or money order for the retail price plus $3.50 s&h to Twilight Times Books, Dept. LS-0408 POB 3340 Kingsport TN 37664. Delivery may take up to three weeks.

Name: _____

Address: _____

_____

Email: _____

I have enclosed a check or money order in the amount of

$_____

for _____ .

Praise for *Awkward Grace*

"...Because of its universal appeal and because there are life lessons to be learned in *Awkward Grace*, which is never, ever preachy in its tone, I recommend this book not only to other adults, but believe it would be suitable for teens as well. There is a positive, uplifting tone throughout the book that can't help but affect the reader for the better."
~ L. L. Woodard, for *Round Table Reviews*

"This is a book about love, but it is not a love story. This is a book about war and hate and genocide, but, as I told you, it is about love. It is a book about God, without being in any way sanctimonious or telling you what you ought to be doing or thinking. It is a beautiful book: its language is like poetry, its characters wonderful, strong and real, its descriptions vivid and graphic. With all that, it has humor that will sometimes have you laughing out loud, at others smiling a bittersweet smile—and yet, it is also an inspirational book that will bring tears to your eyes, no matter how tough you think yourself to be."
~ Dr. Bob Rich, writer, mudsmith, & psychologist

CPSIA information can be obtained at www.ICGtesting.com
Printed in the USA
LVOW092140060612

285027LV00001B/77/P